Robert Cromie

The Crack of Doom

Robert Cromie

The Crack of Doom

ISBN/EAN: 9783337387259

Printed in Europe, USA, Canada, Australia, Japan

Cover: Foto ©Andreas Hilbeck / pixelio.de

More available books at **www.hansebooks.com**

THE CRACK OF DOOM

BY

ROBERT CROMIE

Author of "A Plunge into Space," etc.

SECOND EDITION

LONDON

DIGBY, LONG & CO.

18 BOUVERIE STREET, FLEET STREET, E.C.

1895

PREFACE

THE rough notes from which this narrative has been constructed were given to me by the man who tells the story. For obvious reasons I have altered the names of the principals, and I hereby pass on the assurance which I have received, that the originals of such as are left alive can be found if their discovery be thought desirable. This alteration of names, the piecing together of somewhat disconnected and sometimes nearly indecipherable memoranda, and the reduction of the mass to consecutive form, are all that has been required of me or would have been permitted to me. The expedition to Labrador mentioned by the narrator has not returned, nor has it ever been definitely traced. He does not undertake to prove that it ever set out. But he avers that all which is hereafter set down is truly told, and he leaves it to mankind to accept the warning which it has fallen to him to convey, or await the proof of its sincerity which he believes the end of the century will produce.

ROBERT CROMIE.

BELFAST, *May, 1895.*

CONTENTS

THE CRACK OF DOOM

CHAPTER I

THE UNIVERSE A MISTAKE!

"THE Universe is a mistake!"

Thus spake Herbert Brande, a passenger on the *Majestic*, making for Queenstown Harbour, one evening early in the past year. Foolish as the words may seem, they were partly influential in leading to my terrible association with him, and all that is described in this book.

Brande was standing beside me on the starboard side of the vessel. We had been discussing a current astronomical essay, as we watched the hazy blue line of the Irish coast rise on the horizon. This conversation was interrupted by Brande, who said, impatiently:

"Why tell us of stars distant so far from this

A

insignificant little world of ours—so insignificant that even its own inhabitants speak disrespectfully of it—that it would take hundreds of years to telegraph to some of them, thousands to others, and millions to the rest? Why limit oneself to a mere million of years for a dramatic illustration, when there is a star in space distant so far from us that if a telegram left the earth for it this very night, and maintained for ever its initial velocity, it would never reach that star?"

He said this without any apparent effort after rhetorical effect; but the suddenness with which he had presented a very obvious truism in a fresh light to me made the conception of the vastness of space absolutely oppressive. In the hope of changing the subject I replied :

"Nothing is gained by dwelling on these scientific speculations. The mind is only bewildered. The Universe is inexplicable."

"The Universe!" he exclaimed. "That is easily explained. The Universe is a mistake!"

"The greatest mistake of the century, I suppose," I added, somewhat annoyed, for I thought Brande was laughing at me.

"Say, of Time, and I agree with you," he replied, careless of my astonishment.

I did not answer him for some moments.

This man Brande was young in years, but middle-aged in the expression of his pale, intellectual face, and old—if age be synonymous with knowledge—in his ideas. His knowledge, indeed, was so exhaustive that the scientific pleasantries to which he was prone could always be justified, dialectically at least, by him when he was contradicted. Those who knew him well did not argue with him. I was always stumbling into intellectual pitfalls, for I had only known him since the steamer left New York.

As to myself, there is little to be told. My history prior to my acquaintance with Brande was commonplace. I was merely an active, athletic Englishman, Arthur Marcel by name. I had studied medicine, and was a doctor in all but the degree. This certificate had been dispensed with owing to an unexpected legacy, on receipt of which I determined to devote it to the furtherance of my own amusement. In the pursuit of this object, I had visited many lands and had become familiar with most of the beaten tracks of travel. I was returning to England after an absence of three years spent in aimless roaming. My age was thirty-one years, and my salient characteristic at the time was to hold fast by anything that interested me, until my humour changed. Brande's conversational vagaries had amused me on the voyage. His extraordinary comment on the Universe decided me to cement our shipboard acquaintance before reaching port.

"That explanation of yours," I said, lighting a fresh cigar, and returning to a subject which I had so recently tried to shelve, "isn't it rather vague?"

"For the present it must serve," he answered absently.

To force him into admitting that his phrase was only a thoughtless exclamation, or induce him to defend it, I said:

"It does not serve any reasonable purpose. It adds nothing to knowledge. As it stands, it is neither academic nor practical."

Brande looked at me earnestly for a moment, and then said gravely:

"The academic value of the explanation will be shown to you if you will join a society I have founded; and its practicalness will soon be made plain whether you join or not."

"What do you call this club of yours?" I asked.

" We·do not call it a club. We call it a Society
—the *Cui Bono* Society," he answered coldly.

"I like the name," I returned. " It is
suggestive. It may mean anything—or nothing."

"You will learn later that the Society means
something ; a good deal, in fact."

This was said in the dry, unemotional tone
which I afterwards found was the only sign of
displeasure Brande ever permitted himself to show.
His arrangements for going on shore at Queenstown had been made early in the day, but he left
me to look for his sister, of whom I had seen
very little on the voyage. The weather had been
rough, and as she was not a good sailor, I had
only had a rare glimpse of a very dark and handsome girl, whose society possessed for me a
strange attraction, although we were then almost
strangers. Indeed, I regretted keenly, as the
time of our separation approached, having re-
gistered my luggage (consisting largely of curios
and mementoes of my travels, of which I was
very careful) for Liverpool. My own time was
valueless, and it would have been more agreeable
to me to continue the journey with the Brandes,
no matter where they went.

There was a choppy sea on when we reached

the entrance to the harbour, so the *Majestic* steamed in between the Carlisle and Camden forts, and on to the man-of-war roads, where the tender met us. By this time, Brande and his sister were ready to go on shore; but as there was a heavy mail to be transhipped, we had still an hour at our disposal. For some time we paced the deck, exchanging commonplaces on the voyage and confidences as to our future plans. It was almost dark, but not dark enough to prevent us from seeing those wonderfully green hills which land-lock the harbour. To me the verdant woods and hills were delightful after the brown plains and interminable prairies on which I had spent many months. As the lights of Queenstown began to speck the slowly gathering gloom, Miss Brande asked me to point out Rostellan Castle. It could not be seen from the vessel, but the familiar legend was easily recalled, and this led us to talk about Irish tradition with its weird romance and never failing pathos. This interested her. Freed now from the lassitude of sea-sickness, the girl became more fascinating to me every moment. Everything she said was worth listening to, apart from the charming manner in which it was said.

To declare that she was an extremely pretty

girl would not convey the strange, almost unearthly, beauty of her face—as intellectual as
her brother's—and of the charm of her slight but
exquisitely moulded figure. In her dark eyes
there was a sympathy, a compassion, that was
new to me. It thrilled me with an emotion
different from anything that my frankly happy,
but hitherto wholly selfish life had known. There
was only one note in her conversation which jarred
upon me. She was apt to drift into the extraordinary views of life and death which were
interesting when formulated by her eccentric
brother, but pained me coming from her lips.
In spite of this, the purpose I had contemplated
of joining Brande's Society—evoked as it had
been by his own whimsical observation—now took
definite form. I would join that Society. It
would be the best way of keeping near to Natalie
Brande.

Her brother returned to us to say that the
tender was about to leave the ship. He had left
us for half an hour. I did not notice his absence
until he himself announced it. As we shook
hands, I said to him :

"I have been thinking about that Society of
yours. I mean to join it."

"I am very glad," he replied. "You will find it a new sensation, quite outside the beaten track, which you know so well."

There was a shade of half-kindly contempt in his voice, which missed me at the moment. I answered gaily, knowing that he would not be offended by what was said in jest:

"I am sure I shall. If all the members are as mad as yourself, it will be the most interesting experience outside Bedlam that any man could wish for."

I had a foretaste of that interest soon.

As Miss Brande was walking to the gangway, a lamp shone full upon her gypsy face. The blue-black hair, the dark eyes, and a deep red rose she wore in her bonnet, seemed to me an exquisite arrangement of harmonious colour. And the thought flashed into my mind very vividly, however trivial it may seem here, when written down in cold words: "The queen of women, and the queen of flowers." That is not precisely how my thought ran, but I cannot describe it better. The finer subtleties of the brain do not bear well the daylight of language.

Brande drew her back and whispered to her

Then the sweet face, now slightly flushed, was turned to me again.

"Oh, thank you for that pretty thought," she said with a pleasant smile. "You are too flattering. The 'queen of flowers' is very true, but the 'queen of women!' Oh, no!" She made a graceful gesture of dissent, and passed down the gangway.

As the tender disappeared into the darkness, a tiny scrap of lace waved, and I knew vaguely that she was thinking of me. But how she read my thought so exactly I could not tell.

That knowledge it has been my fate to gain.

CHAPTER II.

A STRANGE EXPERIMENT.

Soon after my arrival in London, I called on
Brande, at the address he had given me in Brook
Street. He received me with the pleasant
affability which a man of the world easily
assumes, and his apology for being unable to
pass the evening with me in his own house was
a model of social style. The difficulty in the
way was practically an impossibility. His
Society had a meeting on that evening, and it
was imperative that he should be present.

"Why not come yourself?" he said. "It is
what we might call a guest night. That is,
visitors, if friends of members, are admitted,
and as this privilege may not be again accorded
to outsiders, you ought to come before you decide
finally to join us. I must go now, but Natalie"
(he did not say "Miss Brande") "will entertain
you and bring you to the hall. It is very near—
in Hanover Square."

"I shall be very glad indeed to bring Miss Brande to the hall," I answered, changing the sentence in order to correct Brande's too patronising phrase.

"The same thing in different words, is it not? If you prefer it that way, please have it so." His imperturbability was unaffected.

Miss Brande here entered the room. Her brother, with a word of renewed apology, left us, and presently I saw him cross the street and hail a passing hansom.

"You must not blame him for running off," Miss Brande said. "He has much to think of, and the Society depends almost wholly on himself."

I stammered out that I did not blame him at all, and indeed my disclaimer was absolutely true. Brande could not have pleased me better than he had done by relieving us of his company.

Miss Brande made tea, which I pretended to enjoy in the hope of pleasing her. Over this we talked more like old and well proven friends than mere acquaintances of ten days' standing. Just once or twice the mysterious chord which marred the girl's charming conversation was touched. She immediately changed the subject

on observing my distress. I say distress, for a
weaker word would not fittingly describe the
emotion I felt whenever she blundered into the
pseudo-scientific nonsense which was her brother's
favourite affectation.   At least, it seemed nonsense to me. I could not well foresee then that
the theses which appeared to be mere theo-
retical absurdities, would ever be proven—as they
have been—very terrible realities.   On subjects
of ordinary educational interest my hostess dis-
played such full knowledge of the question
and ease in dealing with it, that I listened, fascin-
ated, as long as she chose to continue speaking.
It was a novel and delightful experience to hear
a girl as handsome as a pictorial masterpiece,
and dressed like a court beauty, discourse with
the knowledge, and in the language, of the
oldest philosopher.   But this was only one of
the many surprising combinations in her complex
personality.   My noviciate was still in its first
stage.

The time to set out for the meeting arrived
all too soon for my inclination. We decided to
walk, the evening being fine and not too warm,
and the distance only a ten minutes' stroll.   At
a street crossing, we met a crowd unusually

large for that neighbourhood. Miss Brande again surprised me. She was watching the crowd seething and swarming past. Her dark eyes followed the people with a strange wondering, pitying look which I did not understand. Her face, exquisite in its expression at all times, was now absolutely transformed, beatified. Brande had often spoken to me of mesmerism, clairvoyance, and similar subjects, and it occurred to me that he had used his sister as a medium, a clairvoyante. Her brain was not, therefore, under normal control. I determined instantly to tell him on the first opportunity that if he did not wish to see the girl permanently injured, he would have to curtail his hypnotic influence.

" It is rather a stirring sight," I said so sharply to Miss Brande that she started. I meant to startle her, but did not succeed as far as I wished.

" It is a very terrible sight," she answered.

" Oh, there is no danger," I said hastily, and drew her hand over my arm.

" Danger ! I was not thinking of danger."

As she did not remove her hand, I did not infringe the silence which followed this, until a break in the traffic allowed us to cross the street. Then I said :

" May I ask what you were thinking of just now, Miss Brande ? "

" Of the people—their lives—their work— their misery ! "

" I assure you many are very happy," I replied. " You take a morbid view. Misery is not the rule. I am sure the majority are happy."

" What difference does that make ? " the girl said with a sigh. " What is the end of it all—the meaning of it all ? Their happiness ! *Cui Bono ?* "

We walked on in silence, while I turned over in my mind what she had said. I could come to no conclusion upon it save that my dislike for her enigmatic aberrations was becoming more intense as my liking for the girl herself increased. To change the current of her thoughts and my own, I asked her abruptly :

" Are you a member of the *Cui Bono* Society ? "

" I ! Oh, no. Women are not allowed to join—for the present."

" I am delighted to hear it," I said heartily, " and I hope the rule will continue in force."

She looked at me in surprise. "Why should you mind? You are joining yourself."

"That is different. I don't approve of ladies mixing themselves up in these curious and perhaps questionable societies."

My remark amused her. Her eyes sparkled with simple fun. The change in her manner was very agreeable to me.

"I might have expected that." To my extreme satisfaction she now looked almost mischievous. "Herbert told me you were a little—"

" A little what ? "

"Well, a little—you won't be vexed? That is right. He said a little—mediæval."

This abated my appreciation of her sense of humour, and I maintained a dignified reticence, which unhappily she regarded as mere sullenness, until we reached the Society's room.

The place was well filled, and the company, in spite of the extravagantly modern costumes of the younger women, which I cannot describe better than by saying that there was little difference in it from that of ordinary male attire, was quite conventional in so far as the interchange of ordinary courtesies went. When, however, any member of the Society mingled with

a group of visitors, the conversation was soon
turned into a new channel. Secrets of science,
which I had been accustomed to look upon as
undiscoverable, were bandied about like the
merest commonplaces of education. The absurdity of individuality and the subjectivity of
the emotions were alike insisted on without
notice of the paradox, which to me appeared extreme. The Associates were altruistic for the
sake of altruism, not for the sake of its bene-
ficiaries. They were not pantheists, for they
saw neither universal good nor God, but rather
evil in all things—themselves included. Their
talk, however, was brilliant, and, with allowance
for its jarring sentiments, it possessed something
of the indefinable charm which followed Brande.
My reflections on this identity of interest were
interrupted by the man himself. After a word
of welcome he said:

" Let me show you our great experiment; that
which touches the high-water mark of scientific
achievement in the history of humanity. It is
not much in itself, but it is the pioneer of many
marvels."

He brought me to a metal stand, on which a
small instrument constructed of some white metal

was placed. A large number of wires were connected with various portions of it, and these
wires passed into the side - wall of the building.

In appearance, this marvel of micrology, so
far as the eye-piece and upper portions went,
was like an ordinary microscope, but its magnifying power was to me unbelievable. It magnified
the object under examination many thousand
times more than the most powerful microscope
in the world.

I looked through the upper lens, and saw a
small globe suspended in the middle of a tiny
chamber filled with soft blue light, or transparent
material. Circling round this globe four other
spheres revolved in orbits, some almost circular,
some elliptical, some parabolic. As I looked,
Brande touched a key, and the little globules
began to fly more rapidly round their primary,
and make wider sweeps in their revolutions.
Another key was pressed, and the revolving
spheres slowed down and drew closer until I
could scarcely distinguish any movement. The
globules seemed to form a solid ball.

"Attend now!" Brande exclaimed.

He tapped the first key sharply. A little grey

cloud obscured the blue light. When it cleared away, the revolving globes had disappeared.

"What do you think of it?" he asked carelessly.

"What is it? What does it mean? Is it the solar system or some other system illustrated in miniature? I am sorry for the misadventure."

"You are partly correct," Brande replied. "It is an illustration of a planetary system, though a small one. But there was no misadventure. I caused the somewhat dangerous result you witnessed, the wreckage not merely of the molecule of marsh gas you were examining—which any educated chemist might do as easily as I—but the wreckage of its constituent atoms. This is a scientific victory which dwarfs the work of Hermholz, Avogadro, or Mendelejeff. The immortal Dalton himself" (the word "immortal" was spoken with a sneer) "might rise from his grave to witness it."

"Atoms—molecules! What are you talking about?" I asked, bewildered.

"You were looking on at the death of a molecule—a molecule of marsh gas, as I have already said. It was caused by a process which I would describe to you if I could reduce my own life work—and that of every scientific amateur who has preceded me since the world began—into half a dozen sentences. As that would be difficult, I must ask you to accept my personal assurance that you witnessed a fact, not a fiction of my imagination."

"And your instrument is so perfect that it not only renders molecules and atoms but their diffusion visible? It is a microscopic impossibility. At least it is amazing."

"Pshaw!" Brande exclaimed impatiently. "My instrument does certainly magnify to a marvellous extent, but not by the old device of the simple microscope, which merely focussed a large area of light rays into a small one. So crude a process could never show an atom to the human eye. I add much to that. I restore to the rays themselves the luminosity which they lost in their passage through our atmosphere. I give them back all their visual properties, and turn them with their full etheric blaze on the object under examination. Great as that achievement is, I deny that it is amazing. It may amaze a Papuan to see his eyelash magnified to the size of a wire, or an uneducated Englishman to see a cheesemite magnified to the size of a midge. It should not amaze you to see a simple process a little further developed."

"Where does the danger you spoke of come in?" I asked with a pretence of interest. Candidly, I did not believe a single word that Brande had said.

"If you will consult a common text-book on the physics of the ether," he replied, "you will find that one grain of matter contains sufficient energy, if etherised, to raise a hundred thousand tons nearly two miles. In face of such potentiality it is not wise to wreck incautiously even the atoms of a molecule."

"And the limits to this description of scientific experiment? Where are they?"

"There are no limits," Brande said decisively. "No man can say to science 'thus far and no farther.' No man ever has been able to do so. No man ever shall!"

CHAPTER III.

AMONGST the letters lying on my breakfast-table a few days after the meeting was one addressed in an unfamiliar hand. The writing was bold, and formed like a man's. There was a faint trace of a perfume about the envelope which I remembered. I opened it first.

It was, as I expected, from Miss Brande. Her brother had gone to their country place on the southern coast. She and her friend, Edith Metford, were going that day. Their luggage was already at the station. Would I send on what I required for a short visit, and meet them at eleven o'clock on the bridge over the Serpentine? It was enough for me. I packed a large portmanteau hastily, sent it to Charing Cross, and spent the time at my disposal in the park, which was close to my hotel.

Although the invitation I had received gave

21

me pleasure, I could not altogether remove from my mind a vague sense of disquietude concerning Herbert Brande and his Society. The advanced opinions I had heard, if extreme, were not altogether alarming. But the mysterious way in which Brande himself had spoken about the Society, and the still more mysterious air which some of the members assumed when directly questioned as to its object, suggested much. Might it not be a revolutionary party engaged in a grave intrigue — a branch of some foreign body whose purpose was so dangerous that ordinary disguises were not considered sufficiently secure ? Might they not have adopted the jargon and pretended to the opinions of scientific faddists as a cloak for designs more sinister and sincere ? The experiment I witnessed might be almost a miracle or merely a trick. Thinking it over thus, I could come to no final opinion, and when I asked myself aloud, " What are you afraid of ? " I could not answer my own question. But I thought I would defer joining the Society pending further information.

A few minutes before eleven, I walked towards the bridge over the Serpentine. No ladies appeared to be on it. There were only a couple of smartly dressed youths there, one smoking a cigarette. I sauntered about until one of the lads, the one who was not smoking, looked up and beckoned to me. I approached leisurely, for it struck me that the boy would have shown better breeding if he had come toward me, considering my seniority.

"I am sorry I did not notice you sooner. Why did you not come on when you saw us?" the smallest and slimmest youth called to me.

"In the name of—Miss—Miss—" I stammered.

"Brande; you haven't forgotten my name, I hope," Natalie Brande said coolly. "This is my friend, Edith Metford. Metford, this is Arthur Marcel."

"How do you do, Marcel? I am glad to meet you; I have heard 'favourable mention' of you from the Brandes," the second figure in knickerbockers said pleasantly.

"How do you do, sir — madam — I mean— Miss—" I blundered, and then in despair I asked Miss Brande, "Is this a tableau vivant? What is the meaning of these disguises?" My embarrassment was so great that my discourteous question may be pardoned.

"Our dress! Surely you have seen women rationally dressed before!" Miss Brande answered complacently, while the other girl watched my astonishment with evident amusement.

This second girl, Edith Metford, was a frank, handsome young woman, but unlike the spirituelle beauty of Natalie Brande. She was perceptibly taller than her friend, and of fuller figure. In consequence, she looked, in my opinion, to even less advantage in her eccentric costume, or rational dress, than did Miss Brande.

"Rationally dressed! Oh, yes. I know the divided skirt, but—"

Miss Metford interrupted me. "Do you call the divided skirt atrocity rational dress?" she asked pointedly.

"Upon my honour I do not," I answered.

These girls were too advanced in their ideas of dress for me. Nor did I feel at all at my ease during this conversation, which did not, however, appear to embarrass them. I proposed hastily to get a cab, but they demurred. It was such a lovely day, they preferred to walk, part of the way at least. I pointed out that there might be drawbacks to this amendment of my proposal.

"What drawbacks?" Miss Metford asked.

"For instance, isn't it probable we shall all be arrested by the police?" I replied.

"Rubbish! We are not in Russia," both exclaimed.

"Which is lucky for you," I reflected, as we commenced what was to me a most disagreeable walk. I got them into a cab sooner than they wished. At the railway station I did not offer to procure their tickets. To do so, I felt, would only give offence. Critical glances followed us as we went to our carriage. Londoners are becoming accustomed to varieties, if not vagaries, in ladies' costumes, but the dress of my friends was evidently a little out of the common even for them. Miss Metford was just turning the handle of a carriage door, when I interposed, saying, "This is a smoking compartment."

"So I see. I am going to smoke—if you don't object?"

"I don't suppose it would make any difference if I did," I said, with unconscious asperity, for indeed this excess of free manners was jarring upon me. The line dividing it from vulgarity was becoming so thin I was losing sight of the divisor. Yet no one, even the most fastidious, could associate vulgarity with Natalie Brande. There remained an air of unassumed sincerity about herself and all her actions, including even her dress, which absolutely excluded her from hostile criticism. I could not, however, extend that lenient judgment to Miss Metford. The girls spoke and acted—as they had dressed themselves—very much alike. Only, what seemed to me in the one a natural eccentricity, seemed in the other an unnatural affectation.

I saw the guard passing, and, calling him over, gave him half - a - crown to have the compartment labelled, "Engaged."

Miss Brande, who had been looking out of the window, absently asked my reason for this precaution. I replied that I wanted the compartment reserved for ourselves. I certainly did not want any staring and otherwise offensive fellow-passengers.

"We don't want all the seats," she persisted.

"No," I admitted. "We don't want the extra seats. But I thought you might like the privacy."

"The desire for privacy is an archaic emotion," Miss Metford remarked sententiously, as she struck a match.

" Besides, it is so selfish. We may be crowding others," Miss Brande said quietly.

I was glad she did not smoke.

" I don't want that now," I said to a porter who was hurrying up with a label. To the girls I remarked a little snappishly, " Of course you are quite right. You must excuse my ignorance."

" No, it is not ignorance," Miss Brande demurred. " You have been away so much. You have hardly been in England, you told me, for years, and—"

" And progress has been marching in my absence," I interrupted.

" So it seems," Miss Metford remarked so significantly that I really could not help retorting with as much emphasis, compatible with politeness, as I could command :

" You see I am therefore unable to appreciate the New Woman, of whom I have heard so much since I came home."

" The conventional New Woman is a grandmotherly old fossil," Miss Metford said quietly.

This disposed of me. I leant back in my seat, and was rigidly silent.

Miles of green fields stippled with daisies and

bordered with long lines of white and red haw-
thorn hedges flew past. The smell of new-mown
hay filled the carriage with its sweet perfume,
redolent of old associations. My long absence
dwindled to a short holiday. The world's wide
highways were far off. I was back in the English
fields. My slight annoyance passed away. I fell
into a pleasant day-dream, which was broken by a
soft voice, every undulation of which I already
knew by heart.

"I am afraid you think us very advanced," it
murmured.

"Very," I agreed, "but I look to you to bring
even me up to date."

"Oh, yes, we mean to do that, but we must proceed very gradually."

"You have made an excellent start," I put
in.

"Otherwise you would only be shocked."

"It is quite possible." I said this with so much
conviction that the two burst out laughing at me.
I could not think of anything more to add, and I
felt relieved when, with a warning shriek, the
train dashed into a tunnel. By the time we had
emerged again into the sunlight and the solitude
of the open landscape I had ready an impromptu

which I had been working at in the darkness. I looked straight at Miss Metford and said:

"After all, it is very pleasant to travel with girls like you."

"Thank you!"

"You did not show any hysterical fear of my kissing you in the tunnel."

"Why the deuce would you do that?" Miss Metford replied with great composure, as she blew a smoke ring.

When we reached our destination I braced myself for another disagreeable minute or two. For if the great Londoners thought us quaint, surely the little country station idlers would swear we were demented. We crossed the platform so quickly that the wonderment we created soon passed. Our luggage was looked after by a servant, to whose care I confided it with a very brief description. The loss of an item of it did not seem to me of as much importance as our own immediate departure.

Brande met us at his hall door. His house was a pleasant one, covered with flowering creeping plants, and surrounded by miniature forests. In front there was a lake four hundred yards in width. Close-shaven lawns bordered it. They were artificial products, no doubt, but they were artficial successes—undulating, earth-scented, fresh rolled every morning. Here there was an isolated shrub, there a thick bank of rhododendrons. And the buds, bursting into floral carnival, promised fine contrasts when their full splendour was come. The lake wavelets tinkled musically on a pebbly beach.

Our host could not entertain us in person. He was busy. The plea was evidently sincere, notwithstanding that the business of a country gentleman—which he now seemed to be—is something less exacting than busy people's leisure. After a short rest, and an admirably-served lunch, we were dismissed to the woods for our better amusement.

Thereafter followed for me a strangely peaceful, idyllic day—all save its ending. Looking back on it, I know that the sun which set that evening went down on the last of my happiness. But it all seems trivial now.

My companions were accomplished botanists, and here, for the first time, I found myself on common ground with both. We discussed every familiar wild flower as eagerly as if we had been professed field naturalists. In walking or climbing

my assistance was neither requisitioned nor required. I did not offer, therefore, what must
have been unwelcome when it was superfluous.

We rested at last under the shade of a big
beech, for the afternoon sun was rather oppressive. It was a pleasant spot to while away an
hour. A purling brook went babbling by, singing
to itself as it journeyed to the sea. Insects droned
about in busy flight. There was a perfume of
honeysuckle wafted to us on the summer wind,
which stirred the beech-tree and rustled its young
leaves lazily, so that the sunlight peeped through
the green lattice-work and shone on the faces of
these two handsome girls, stretched in graceful
postures on the cool sward below—their white
teeth sparkling in its brilliance, while their soft
laughter made music for me. In the fulness of
my heart, I said aloud:

" It is a good thing to be alive."

CHAPTER IV.

"It is a good thing to be alive," Natalie Brande repeated slowly, gazing, as it were, far off through her half-closed eyelids. Then turning to me and looking at me full, wide-eyed, she asked: "A good thing for how many?"

"For all; for everything that is alive."

"Faugh! For few things that are alive. For hardly anything. You say it is a good thing to be alive. How often have you said that in your life?"

"All my life through," I answered stoutly. My constitution was a good one, and I had lived healthily, if hardily. I voiced the superfluous vitality of a well nourished body.

"Then you do not know what it is to feel for others."

There was a scream in the underwood near us. It ended in a short, choking squeak. The girl paled, but she went on with outward calm.

32

"That hawk or cat feels as you do. I wonder what that young rabbit thinks of life's problem ? "

"But we are neither hawks nor cats, nor even young rabbits," I answered warmly. "We can not bear the burthens of the whole animal world. Our own are sufficient for us."

"You are right. They are more than sufficient."

I had made a false move, and so tried to recover my lost ground. She would not permit me. The conversation which had run in pleasant channels for two happy hours was ended Thenceforth, in spite of my obstructive efforts, subjects were introduced which could not be conversed on but must be discussed. On every one Miss Brande took the part of the weak against the strong, oblivious of every consideration of policy and even ethics, careful only that she championed the weak because of their weakness. Miss Metford abetted her in this, and went further in their joint revolt against common sense. Miss Brande was argumentative, pleading. Miss Metford was defiant. Between the two I fared ill.

Of course the Woman question was soon introduced, and in this I made the best defence of time-honoured customs of which I was capable. But my outworks fell down as promptly before the voices of these young women as did the walls of Jericho before the blast of a ram's horn. Nothing that I had cherished was left to me. Woman no longer wanted man's protection. ("Enslavement" they called it.) Why should she, when in the evolution of society there was not now, or presently would not be, anything from which to protect her? ("Competing slaveowners" was what they said.) When you wish to behold protectors you must postulate dangers. The first are valueless save as a preventive of the second. Both evils will be conveniently dispensed with. All this was new to me, most of my thinking life having been passed in distant lands, where the science of ethics is codified into a simple statute—the will of the strongest.

When my dialectical humiliation was within one point of completion, Miss Metford came to my rescue. For some time she had looked on at my discomfiture with a good-natured neutrality, and when I was metaphorically in my last ditch, she arose, stretched her shapely figure, flicked some clinging grass blades from her suit, and declared it was time to return. Brande was a man of science, but as such he was still amenable to punctuality in the matter of dinner.

On the way back I was discreetly silent. When we reached the house I went to look for Herbert Brande. He was engaged in his study, and I could not intrude upon him there. To do so would be to infringe the only rigid rule in his household. Nor had I an opportunity of speaking to him alone until after dinner, when I induced him to take a turn with me round the lake. I smoked strong cigars, and made one of these my excuse.

The sun was setting when we started, and as we walked slowly the twilight shadows were deepening fast by the time we reached the further shore. Brande was in high spirits. Some new scientific experiment, I assumed, had come off successfully. He was beside himself. His conversation was volcanic. Now it rumbled and roared with suppressed fires. Anon, it burst forth in scintillating flashes and shot out streams of quickening wit. I have been his auditor in the three great epochs of his life, but I do not think that anything that I have recollected of his utterances equals the bold impromptus, the masterly handling of his favourite subject, the

Universe, which fell from him on that evening. I could not answer him. I could not even follow him, much less suppress him. But I had come forth with a specific object in view, and I would not be gainsaid. And so, as my business had to be done better that it should be done quickly. Taking advantage of a pause which he made, literally for breath, I commenced abruptly:

" I want to speak to you about your sister."

He turned on me surprised. Then his look changed to one of such complete contempt, and withal his bearing suggested so plainly that he knew beforehand what I was going to say, that I blurted out defiantly, and without stopping to choose my words:

" I think it an infernal shame that you, her brother, should allow her to masquerade about with this good-natured but eccentric Metford girl —I should say Miss Metford."

" Why so ? " he asked coldly.

"Because it is absurd; and because it isn't decent."

" My dear Abraham," Brande said quietly, " or is your period so recent as that of Isaac or Jacob ? My sister pleases herself in these matters, and has every right to do so."

" She has not. You are her brother."

" Very well, I am her brother. She has no right to think for herself; no right to live save by my permission. Then I graciously permit her to think, and I allow her to live."

"You'll be sorry for this nonsense sooner or later—and don't say I didn't warn you." The absolute futility of my last clause struck me painfully at the moment, but I could not think of any way to better it. It was hard to reason with such a man, one who denied the fundamental principles of family life. I was thinking over what to say next, when Brande stopped and put his hand, in a kindly way, upon my shoulder.

" My good fellow," he said, " what does it matter? What do the actions of my sister signify more than the actions of any other man's sister? And what about the Society? Have you made up your mind about joining ? "

" I have. I made it up twice to day," I answered. " I made it up in the morning that I would see yourself and your Society to the devil before I would join it. Excuse my bluntness ; but you are so extremely candid yourself you will not mind."

"Certainly, I do not mind bluntness. Rudeness is superfluous."

"And I made it up this evening," I said, a little less aggressively, "that I would join it if the devil himself were already in it, as I half suspect he is."

"I like that," Brande said gravely. "That is the spirit I want in the man who joins me."

To which I replied: "What under the sun is the object of this Society of yours?"

"Proximately to complete our investigations— already far advanced—into the origin of the Universe."

"And ultimately?"

"I cannot tell you now. You will not know that until you join us."

"And if your ultimate object does not suit me, I can withdraw?"

"No, it would then be too late."

"How so? I am not morally bound by an oath which I swear without full knowledge of its consequences and responsibilities."

"Oath! The oath you swear! You swear no oath. Do you fancy you are joining a society of Rechabites or Carmelites, or mediæval rubbish

of that kind. Don't keep so painstakingly behind the age."

I thought for a moment over what this mysterious man had said, over the hidden dangers
in which his mad chimeras might involve the
most innocent accomplice. Then I thought of
that dark-eyed, sweet-voiced, young girl, as
she lay on the green grass under the beech-
tree in the wood and out-argued me on every
point. Very suddenly, and, perhaps, in a manner
somewhat grandiose, I answered him:

"I will join your Society for my own purpose, and I will quit it when I choose."

"You have every right," Brande said carelessly. "Many have done the same before
you."

"Can you introduce me to any one who has
done so?" I asked, with an eagerness that could
not be dissembled.

"I am afraid I can not."

"Or give me an address?"

"Oh yes, that is simple." He turned over a
note-book until he found a blank page. Then
he drew the pencil from its loop, put the point
to his lips, and paused. He was standing with
his back to the failing light, so I could not

see the expression of his mobile face. When
he paused, I knew that no ordinary doubt be-
set him. He stood thus for nearly a minute.
While he waited, I watched a pair of swans
flit ghost-like over the silken surface of the
lake. Between us and a dark bank of wood
the lights of the house flamed red. The melancholy even-song of a blackbird wailed out from
a shrubbery beside us. Then Herbert Brande
wrote in his note-book, and tearing out the
page, he handed it to me, saying: "That is
the address of the last man who quitted us."

The light was now so dim I had to hold
the paper close to my eyes in order to read
the lines. They were these—

GEORGE DELANY,
    Near Saint Anne's Chapel,
        Woking Cemetery.

CHAPTER V.

THE MURDER CLUB.

"DELANY was the last man who quitted us—you see I use your expression again. I like it," Brande said quietly, watching me as he spoke.

I stood staring at the slip of paper which I held in my hand for some moments before I could reply. When my voice came back, I asked hoarsely:

"Did this man, Delany, die suddenly after quitting the Society?"

"He died immediately. The second event was contemporaneous with the first."

"And in consequence of it?"

"Certainly."

"Have all the members who retired from your list been equally shortlived?"

"Without any exception whatever."

"Then your Society, after all your high-flown talk about it, is only a vulgar murder club," I said bitterly.

"Wrong in fact, and impertinent in its expression. It is not a murder club, and—well, you are the first to discover its vulgarity."

"I call things by their plain names. You may call your Society what you please. As to my joining it in face of what you have told me—"

"Which is more than was ever told to any man before he joined—to any man living or dead. And more, you need not join it yet unless you still wish to do so. I presume what I have said will prevent you."

"On the contrary, if I had any doubt, or if there was any possibility of my wavering before this interview, there is none now. I join at once."

He would have taken my hand, but that I could not permit. I left him without another word, or any form of salute, and returned to the house. I did not appear again in the domestic circle that evening, for I had enough upon my mind without further burdening myself with social pretences.

I sat in my room and tried once more to consider my position. It was this: for the sake of a girl whom I had only met some score of times ; who sometimes acted, talked, dressed after a fashion suggestive of insanity; who had glorious dark eyes, a perfect figure, and an exquisitely beautiful face—but I interrupt myself. For the sake of this girl, and for the manifestly impossible purpose of protecting her from herself as well as others, I had surrendered myself to the probable vengeance of a band of cut-throats if I betrayed them, and to the certain vengeance of the law if I did not. Brande, notwithstanding his constant scepticism, was scrupulously truthful. His statement of fact must be relied upon. His opinions were another matter. As nothing practical resulted from my reflections, I came to the conclusion that I had got into a pretty mess for the sake of a handsome face. I regretted this result, but was glad of the cause of it. On this I went to bed.

Next morning I was early astir, for I must see Natalie Brande without delay, and I felt sure she would be no sluggard on that splendid summer day. I tried the lawn between the house and the lake shore. I did not find her there. I found her friend Miss Metford. The girl was sauntering about, swinging a walking-

cane carelessly. She was still rationally dressed,
but I observed with relief that the rational
part of her costume was more in the nature of
the divided skirt than the plain knickerbockers
of the previous day. She accosted me cheerfully
by my surname, and not to be outdone by her, I
said coolly :

"How d'ye do, Metford ? "

"Very well, thanks. I suppose you expected
Natalie ? You see you have only me."

"Delighted," I was commencing with a forced
smile, when she stopped me.

"You look it. But that can't be helped.
Natalie saw you going out, and sent me to meet
you. I am to look after you for an hour or
so. You join the Society this evening, I hear.
You must be very pleased—and flattered."

I could not assent to this, and so remained
silent. The girl chattered on in her own out-
spoken manner, which, now that I was growing
accustomed to it, I did not find as unpleasant
as at first. One thing was evident to me. She
had no idea of the villainous nature of
Brande's Society. She could not have spoken
so carelessly if she shared my knowledge of it.
While she talked to me, I wondered if it was

fair to her—a likeable girl, in spite of her un-
desirable affectations of advanced opinion, emanci-
pation or whatever she called it—was it fair
to allow her to associate with a band of murderers,
and not so much as whisper a word of warning?
No doubt, I myself was associating with the
band; but I was not in ignorance of the responsi-
bility thereby incurred.

"Miss Metford," I said, without heeding whether
I interrupted her, "are you in the secret of this
Society?"

"I? Not at present. I shall be later on."

I stopped and faced her with so serious an
expression that she listened to me attentively.

"If you will take my earnest advice—and I beg
you not to neglect it—you will have nothing to
do with it or any one belonging to it."

"Not even Brande—I mean Natalie? Is she
dangerous?"

I disregarded her mischief and continued:
"If you can get Miss Brande away from her
brother and his acquaintances," (I had nearly
said accomplices,) "and keep her away, you would
be doing the best and kindest thing you ever
did in your life."

Miss Metford was evidently impressed by my

seriousness, but, as she herself said very truly, it was unlikely that she would be able to interfere in the way I suggested. Besides, my mysterious warning was altogether too vague to be of any use as a guide for her own action, much less that of her friend. I dared not speak plainer. I could only repeat, in the most emphatic words, my anxiety that she would think carefully over what I had said. I then pretended to recollect an engagement with Brande, for I was in such low spirits I had really little taste for any company.

She was disappointed, and said so in her usual straightforward way. It was not in the power of any gloomy prophecy to oppress her long. The serious look which my words had brought on her face passed quickly, and it was in her natural manner that she bade me good - morning, saying :

" It is rather a bore, for I looked forward to a pleasant hour or two taking you about."

I postponed my breakfast for want of appetite, and, as Brande's house was the best example of Liberty Hall I had. ever met with, I offered no apology for my absence during the entire day when I rejoined my host and hostess in the evening. The interval I spent in the woods, thinking much and deciding nothing.

After dinner, Brande introduced me to a man whom he called Edward Grey. Natalie conducted me to the room in which they were engaged. From the mass of correspondence in which this man Grey was absorbed, and the litter of papers about him, it was evident that he must have been in the house long before I made his acquaintance.

Grey handed me a book, which I found to be a register of the names of the members of Brande's Society, and pointed out the place for my signature.

When I had written my name on the list I said to Brande : "Now that I have nominated myself, I suppose you'll second me ?"

"It is not necessary," he answered ; "you are already a member. Your remark to Miss Metford this morning made you one of us. You advised her, you recollect, to beware of us."

"That girl!" I exclaimed, horrified. "Then she is one of your spies? Is it possible ?"

"No, she is not one of our spies. We have none, and she knew nothing of the purpose for which she was used."

" Then I beg to say that you have made a d—d shameful use of her."

In the passion of the moment I forgot my manners to my host, and formed the resolution to denounce the Society to the police the moment I returned to London. Brande was not offended by my violence. There was not a trace of anger in his voice as he said:

" Miss Metford's information was telepathically conveyed to my sister."

" Then it was your sister—"

" My sister knows as little as the other. In turn, I received the information telepathically from her, without the knowledge of either. I was just telling Grey of it when you came into the room."

" And," said Grey, " your intention to go straight from this house to Scotland Yard, there to denounce us to the police, has been telepathically received by myself."

" My God!" I cried, " has a man no longer the right to his own thoughts?"

Grey went on without noticing my exclamation: " Any overt or covert action on your part, toward carrying out your intention, will be telepathically conveyed to us, and our executive—" He shrugged his shoulders.

"I know," I said, "Woking Cemetery, near Saint Anne's Chapel. You have ground there."

"Yes, we have to dispense with—"

"Say murder."

"Dispense with," Grey repeated sharply, "any member whose loyalty is questionable. This is not our wish; it is our necessity. It is the only means by which we can secure the absolute immunity of the Society pending the achievement of its object. To dispense with any living man we have only to will that he shall die."

"And now that I am a member, may I ask what is this object, the secret of which you guard with such fiendish zeal?" I demanded angrily.

"The restoration of a local etheric tumour to its original formation."

"I am already weary of this jargon from Brande," I interrupted. "What do you mean?"

"We mean to attempt the reduction of the solar system to its elemental ether."

"And you will accomplish this triviality by means of Huxley's comet, I suppose?"

I could scarcely control my indignation. This fooling, as I thought it, struck me as insulting. Neither Brande nor Grey appeared to

D

notice my keen resentment. Grey answered me in a quiet, serious tone.

"We shall attempt it by destroying the earth. We may fail in the complete achievement of our design, but in any case we shall at least be certain of reducing this planet to the ether of which it is composed."

"Of course, of course," I agreed derisively. "You will at least make sure of that. You have found out how to do it too, I have no doubt ?"

"Yes," said Grey, "we have found out."

CHAPTER VI.

A TELEPATHIC TELEGRAM.

I LEFT the room and hurried outside without any positive plan for my movements. My brain was in such a whirl I could form no connected train of thought. These men, whose conversation was a jargon fitting only for lunatics, had proved that they could read my mind with the ease of a telegraph operator taking a message off a wire. That they, further, possessed marvellous, if not miraculous powers, over occult natural forces could hardly be doubted. The net in which I had voluntarily entangled myself was closing around me. An irresistible impulse to fly—to desert Natalie and save myself—came over me. I put this aside presently. It was both unworthy and unwise. For whither should I fly? The ends of the earth would not be far enough to save me, the depths of the sea would not be deep

enough to hide me from those who killed by
willing that their victim should die.

On the other hand, if my senses had only been
hocussed, and Messrs. Brande and Grey were
nothing better than clever tricksters, the park
gate was far enough, and the nearest policeman
force enough, to save me from their vengeance.
But the girl—Natalie! She was clairvoyante.
They practised upon her. My diagnosis of the
strange seeing-without-sight expression of her
eyes was then correct. And it was clear to me
that whatsoever or whomsoever Brande and Grey
believed or disbelieved in, they certainly believed
in themselves. They might be relied on to spare
nothing and no one in their project, however
ridiculous or mad their purpose might be. What
then availed my paltry protection when the girl
herself was a willing victim, and the men omni-
potent? Nevertheless, if I failed eventually to
serve her, I could at least do my best.

It was clear that I must stand by Natalie
Brande.

While I was thus reflecting, the following conversation took place between Brande and Grey.
I found a note of it in a diary which Brande
kept desultorily. He wrote this up so irregularly

no continuous information can be gleaned from it
as to his life. How the diary came into my hands
will be seen later. The memorandum is written
thus :—

Grey—Our new member ? Why did you introduce him ? You say he cannot help with
money. It is plain he cannot help with brains.

Brande—He interests Natalie. He is what the
uneducated call good-natured He enjoys doing
unselfish things, unaware that it is for the selfish
sake of the agreeable sensation thereby secured.
Besides, I like him myself. He amuses me. To
make him a member was the only safe way of
keeping him so much about us. But Natalie is
the main reason. I am afraid of her wavering in
spite of my hypnotic influence. In a girl of her
intensely emotional nature the sentiment of hopeless love will create profound melancholy. Dominated by that she is safe. It seems cruel at first
sight. It is not really so. It is not cruel to
reconcile her to a fate she cannot escape. It is
merciful. For the rest, what does it matter ? It
will be all the same in—

Grey—This day six months.

Brande—I believe I shivered. Heredity has
much to answer for.

That is the whole of the entry. I did not read the words until the hand that wrote them was dust.

Natalie professed some disappointment when I announced my immediate return to town. I was obliged to manufacture an excuse for such a hasty departure, and so fell back on an old engagement which I had truly overlooked, and which really called me away. But it would have called long enough without an answer if it had not been for Brande himself, his friend Grey, and their insanities. My mind was fixed on one salient issue : how to get Natalie Brande out of her brother's evil influence. This would be better compassed when I myself was outside the scope of his extraordinary influence. And so I went without delay.

For some time after my return to London, I went about visiting old haunts and friends. I soon tired of this. The haunts had lost their interest. The friends were changed, or I was changed. I could not resume the friendships which had been interrupted. The chain of connection had been broken and the links would not weld easily. So, after some futile efforts to return to the circle I had long deserted, I desisted

and accepted my exclusion with serenity. I am
not sure that I desired the old relationships re-
established. And as my long absence had prevented any fresh shoots of friendship being grafted,
I found myself alone in London. I need say no
more.

One evening I was walking through the streets
in a despondent mood, as had become my habit.
By chance I read the name of a street into which
I had turned to avoid a more crowded thorough-
fare. It was that in which Miss Metford lived. I
knew that she had returned to town, for she
had briefly acquainted me with the fact on a post-
card written some days previously.

Here was a chance of distraction. This girl's
spontaneous gaiety, which I found at first dis-
pleasing, was what I wanted to help me to shake
off the gloomy incubus of thought oppressing me.
It was hardly within the proprieties to call upon
her at such an hour, but it could not matter very
much, when the girl's own ideas were so uncon-
ventional. She had independent means, and lived
apart from her family in order to be rid of
domestic limitations. She had told me that she
carried a latch-key—indeed she had shown it to
me with a flourish of triumph—and that she

delighted in free manners. Free manners, she was careful to add, did not mean bad manners. To my mind the terms were synonymous. When opposite her number I decided to call, and, having knocked at the door, was told that Miss Metford was at home.

"Hallo, Marcel! Glad to see you," she called out, somewhat stridently for my taste. Her dress was rather mannish, as usual. In lieu of her out-door tunic she wore a smoking-jacket. When I entered she was sitting in an arm-chair, with her feet on a music-stool. She arose so hastily that the music-stool was overturned, and allowed to lie where it fell.

"What is the matter?" she asked, concerned. "Have you seen a ghost?"

"I think I have seen many ghosts of late," I said, "and they have not been good company. I was passing your door, and I have come in for comfort."

She crossed the room and poured out some whisky from a decanter which was standing on a side-board. Then she opened a bottle of soda-water with a facility which suggested practice. I was relieved to think that it was not Natalie who was my hostess. Handing me the glass, she said peremptorily :

" Drink that. That is right. Give me the glass. Now smoke. Do I allow smoking here? Pah! I smoke here myself."

I lit a cigar and sat down beside her. The clouds began to lift from my brain and float off in the blue smoke wreaths. We talked on ordinary topics without my once noticing how deftly they had been introduced by Miss Metford. I never thought of the flight of time until a chime from a tiny clock on the mantelpiece—an exquisite sample of the tasteful furniture of the whole room —warned me that my visit had lasted two hours. I arose reluctantly.

She rallied me on my ingratitude. I had come in a sorry plight. I was now restored. She was no longer useful, therefore I left her. And so on, till I said with a solemnity no doubt lugubrious:

"I am most grateful, Miss Metford. I cannot tell you how grateful I am. You would not understand—"

"Oh, please leave my poor understanding alone, and tell me what has happened to you. I should like to hear it. And what is more, I like you." She said this so carelessly, I did not feel embarrassed. " Now, then, the whole story, please." Saying which, she sat down again.

"Do you really know nothing more of Brande's Society than you admitted when I last spoke to you about it?" I asked, without taking the chair she pushed over to me.

"This is all I know," she answered, in the rhyming voice of a young pupil declaiming a piece of a little understood and less cared for recitation. "The society has very interesting evenings. Brande shows one beautiful experiments, which, I daresay, would be amazingly instructive if one were inclined that way, which I am not. The men are mostly long-haired creatures with spectacles. Some of them are rather good-looking. All are wholly mad. And my friend—I mean the only girl I could ever stand as a friend—Natalie Brande, is crazy about them."

"Nothing more than that?"

"Nothing more."

The clock now struck the hour of nine, the warning chime for which had startled me.

"Is there anything more than that?" Miss Metford asked with some impatience.

I thought for a moment. Unless my own senses had deceived me that evening in Brande's house, I ran a great risk of sharing George Delany's fate if I remained where I was much longer. And suppose I told her all I knew, would not that bring the same danger upon her too? So I had to answer:

" I cannot tell you. I am a member now."

" Then you must know more than any mere outsider like myself. I suppose it would not be fair to ask you. Anyhow, you will come back and see me soon. By the way, what is your address? "

I gave her my address. She wrote it down on a silver-cased tablet, and remarked:

" That will be all right. I'll look you up some evening."

As I drove to my hotel, I felt that the mesmeric trick, or whatever artifice had been practised upon me by Brande and Grey, had now assumed its true proportion. I laughed at my fears, and was thankful that I had not described them to the strong-minded young woman to whose kindly society I owed so much. What an idiot she would have thought me!

A servant met me in the hall.

" Telegram, sir. Just arrived at this moment."

I took the telegram, and went upstairs with it unopened in my hand. A strange fear overcame me. I dared not open the envelope. I knew beforehand who the sender was, and what the drift of the message would be. I was right. It was from Brande.

"I beg you to be more cautious. Your discussion with Miss M. this evening might have been disastrous. I thought all was over at nine o'clock.

"BRANDE."

I sat down stupefied. When my senses returned, I looked at the table where I had thrown the telegram. It was not there, nor in the room. I rang for the man who had given it to me, and he came immediately.

"About that telegram you gave me just now, Phillips—"

"I beg your pardon, sir," the man interrupted, "I did not give you any telegram this evening."

"I mean when you spoke to me in the hall."

"Yes, sir. I said 'good-night,' but you took no notice. Excuse me, sir, I thought you looked strange."

"Oh, I was thinking of something else. And I remember now, it was Johnson who gave me the telegram."

"Johnson left yesterday, sir."

"Then it was yesterday I was thinking of. You may go, Phillips."

So Brande's telepathic power was objective as well as subjective. My own brain, unaccustomed to be impressed by another mind "otherwise than through the recognised channels of sense," had supplied the likeliest authority for its message. The message was duly delivered, but the telegram was a delusion.

CHAPTER VII.

GUILTY!

As to protecting Natalie Brande from her brother and the fanatics with whom he associated, it was now plain that I was powerless. And what guarantee had I that she herself was unaware of his nefarious purpose; that she did not sympathise with it? This last thought flashed upon me one day, and the sting of pain that followed it was so intolerable, I determined instantly to prove its falsity or truth.

I telegraphed to Brande that I was running down to spend a day or two with him, and followed my message without waiting for a reply. I have still a very distinct recollection of that journey, notwithstanding much that might well have blotted it from my memory. Every mile sped over seemed to mark one more barrier passed on my way to some strange fate; every moment which brought me nearer this incom-

prehensible girl with her magical eyes was an
epoch of impossibility against my ever voluntarily
turning back. And now that it is all over, I
am glad that I went on steadfastly to the
end.

Brande received me with the easy affability
of a man to whom good breeding had ceased to
be a habit, and had become an instinct. Only
once did anything pass between us bearing on
the extraordinary relationship which he had
established with me—the relation of victor and
victim, I considered it. We had been left together for a few moments, and I said as soon as
the others were out of hearing distance :

" I got your message."

" I know you did," he replied. That was all.
There was an awkward pause. It must be broken
somehow. Any way out of the difficulty was
better than to continue in it.

" Have you seen this ? " I asked, handing Brande
a copy of a novel which I had picked up at a
railway bookstall. When I say that it was new
and popular, it will be understood that it was
indecent.

He looked at the title, and said indifferently :
" Yes, I have seen it, and in order to appreciate

this class of fiction fairly, I have even tried to read it. Why do you ask?"

"Because I thought it would be in your line. It is very advanced." I said this to gain time.

"Advanced—advanced? I am afraid I do not comprehend. What do you mean by 'advanced'? And how could it be in my line. I presume you mean by that, on my plane of thought?"

"By 'advanced,' I mean up-to-date. What do you mean by it?"

"If I used the word at all, I should mean educated, evolved. Is this evolved? Is it even educated? It is not always grammatical. It has no style. In motive, it ante-dates Boccacio."

"You disapprove of it."

"Certainly not."

"Then you approve it, notwithstanding your immediate. condemnation?"

"By no means. I neither approve nor disapprove. It only represents a phase of humanity—the deliberate purpose of securing money or notoriety to the individual, regardless of the welfare of the community. There is nothing to admire in that. It would be invidious to blame it when the whole social scheme is equally wrong and contemptible. By the way, what interest do you think the wares of any literary pander, of either sex, could possess for me, a student— even if a mistaken one—of science ? "

" I did not think the book would possess the slightest interest for you, and I suppose you are already aware of that ? "

" Ah no! My telepathic power is reserved for more serious purposes. Its exercise costs me too much to expend it on trifles. In consequence I do not know why you mentioned the book."

To this I answered candidly, " I mentioned it in order to get myself out of a conversational difficulty—without much success."

Natalie was reserved with me at first. She devoted herself unnecessarily to a boy named Halley who was staying with them. Grey had gone to London. His place was taken by a Mr. Rockingham, whom I did not like. There was something sinister in his expression, and he rarely spoke save to say something cynical, and in conse- quence disagreeable. He had " seen life," that is, everything deleterious to and destructive of it. His connection with Brande was clearly a rebound, the rebound of disgust. There was nothing credit- able to him in that. My first impression of him was thus unfavourable. My last recollection of

E

him is a fitting item in the nightmare which contains it.

The youth Halley would have interested me under ordinary circumstances. His face was as handsome and refined as that of a pretty girl. His figure, too, was slight and his voice effeminate. But there my own advantage, as I deemed it, over him ceased. Intellectually, he was a pupil of Brande's who did his master credit. Having made this discovery I did not pursue it. My mind was fixed too fast upon a definite issue to be more than temporarily interested in the epigrams of a peachy-cheeked man of science.

The afternoon was well advanced before I had an opportunity of speaking to Natalie. When it came, I did not stop to puzzle over a choice of phrases.

"I wish to speak to you alone on a subject of extreme importance to me," I said hurriedly. "Will you come with me to the sea-shore? Your time, I know, is fully occupied. I would not ask this if my happiness did not depend upon it."

The philosopher looked on me with grave, kind eyes. But the woman's heart within her sent the red blood flaming to her cheeks. It was then given to me to fathom the lowest depth of boorish stupidity I had ever sounded.

"I don't mean that," I cried, "I would not dare—"

The blush on her cheek burnt deeper as she tossed her head proudly back, and said straight out, without any show of fence or shadow of concealment:

"It was my mistake. I am glad to know that I did you an injustice. You are my friend, are you not?"

"I believe I have the right to claim that title," I answered.

"Then what you ask is granted. Come." She put her hand boldly into mine. I grasped the slender fingers, saying:

"Yes, Natalie, some day I will prove to you that I am your friend."

"The proof is unnecessary," she replied, in a low sad voice.

We started for the sea. Not a word was spoken on the way. Nor did our eyes meet. We were in a strange position. It was this: the man who had vowed he was the woman's friend—who did not intend to shirk the proof of his promise, and never did gainsay it—meant to ask the woman, before the day was over, to clear herself of knowingly associating with a gang of scientific murderers. The woman had vaguely divined his purpose, and could not clear herself.

When we arrived at the shore we occupied ourselves inconsequently. We hunted little fishes until Natalie's dainty boots were dripping. We examined quaint denizens of the shallow water until her gloves were spoilt. We sprang from rock to rock and evaded the onrush of the foaming waves. We made aqueducts for inter-communication between deep pools. We basked in the sunshine, and listened to the deep moan of the sounding sea, and the solemn murmur of the shells. We drank in the deep breath of the ocean, and for a brief space we were like happy children.

The end came soon to this ephemeral happiness. It was only one of those bright coins snatched from the niggard hand of Time which must always be paid back with usurious charges. We paid with cruel interest.

Standing on a flat rock side by side, I nerved myself to ask this girl the same question I had asked her friend, Edith Metford, how much she knew of the extraordinary and preposterous

Society—as I still tried to consider it—which Herbert Brande had founded. She looked so frank, so refined, so kind, I hardly dared to put my brutal question to an innocent girl, whom I had seen wince at the suffering of a maimed bird, and pale to the lips at the death-cry of a rabbit. This time there was no possibility of untoward consequence in the question save to myself—for surely the girl was safe from her own brother. And I myself preferred to risk the consequences rather than endure longer the thought that she belonged voluntarily to a vile murder club. Yet the question would not come. A simple thing brought it out. Natalie, after looking seaward silently for some minutes, said simply :

"How long are we to stand here, I wonder ?"

"Until you answer this question. How much do you know about your brother's Society, which I have joined to my own intense regret ?"

"I am sorry you regret having joined," she replied gravely.

"You would not be sorry," said I, "if you knew as much about it as I do," forgetting that I had still no answer to my question, and that the extent of her knowledge was unknown to me.

"I believe I do know as much as you." There was a tremor in her voice and an anxious pleading look in her eyes. This look maddened me. Why should she plead to me unless she was guilty? I stamped my foot upon the rock without noticing that in so doing I kicked our whole collection of shells into the water.

There was something more to ask, but I stood silent and sullen. The woods above the beach were choral with bird-voices. They were hateful to me. The sea song of the tumbling waves was hideous. I cursed the yellow sunset light glaring on their snowy crests. A tiny hand was laid upon my arm. I writhed under its deadly if delicious touch. But I could not put it away, nor keep from turning to the sweet face beside me, to mark once more its mute appeal—now more than mere appeal; it was supplication that was in her eyes. Her red lips were parted as though they voiced an unspoken prayer. At last a prayer did pass from them to me.

"Do not judge me until you know me better. Do not hate me without cause. I am not wicked, as you think. I—I—I am trying to do what I think is right. At least, I am not selfish or cruel. Trust me yet a little while."

I looked at her one moment, and then with a sob I clasped her in my arms, and cried aloud:

"My God! to name murder and that angel face in one breath! Child, you have been befooled. You know nothing."

For a second she lingered in my embrace. Then she gently put away my arms, and looking up at me, said fearlessly but sorrowfully:

" I cannot lie—even for your love. I know *all*."

CHAPTER VIII.

THE WOKING MYSTERY.

SHE knew all. Then she was a murderess—or in sympathy with murderers. My arms fell from her. I drew back shuddering. I dared not look in her lying eyes, which cried pity when her base heart knew no mercy. Surely now I had solved the maddening puzzle which the character of this girl had, so far, presented to me. Yet the true solution was as far from me as ever. Indeed, I could not well have been further from it than at that moment.

As we walked back, Natalie made two or three unsuccessful attempts to lure me out of the silence which was certainly more eloquent on my part than any words I could have used. Once she commenced :

" It is hard to explain—"

I interrupted her harshly. " No explanation is possible."

On that she put her handkerchief to her eyes, and a half-suppressed sob shook her slight figure. Her grief distracted me. But what could I say to assuage it ?

At the hall door I stopped and said, "Good-bye."

"Are you not coming in ? "

There was a directness and emphasis in the question which did not escape me.

" I ? " The horror in my own voice surprised myself, and assuredly did not pass without her notice.

"Very well ; good-bye. We are not exactly slaves of convention here, but you are too far advanced in that direction even for me. This is your second startling departure from us. I trust you will spare me the humiliation entailed by the condescension of your further acquaintance."

" Give me an hour ! " I exclaimed aghast. " You do not make allowance for the enigma in which everything is wrapped up. I said I was your friend when I thought you of good report. Give me an hour—only an hour—to say whether I will stand by my promise, now that you yourself have claimed that your report is not good but evil. For that is really what you have protested. Do I ask too much ? or is your generosity more limited even than my own ? "

" Ah, no ! I would not have you think that. Take an hour, or a year—an hour only if you care for my happiness."

" Agreed," said I. " I will take the hour. Discretion can have the year."

So I left her. I could not go indoors. A roof would smother me. Give me the open lawns, the leafy woods, the breath of the summer wind. Away, then, to the silence of the coming night. For an hour leave me to my thoughts. Her unworthiness was now more than suspected. It was admitted. My misery was complete. But I would not part with her; I could not. Innocent or guilty, she was mine. I must suffer with her or for her. The resolution by which I have abided was formed as I wandered lonely through the woods.

When I reached my room that night I found a note from Brande. To receive a letter from a man in whose house I was a guest did not surprise me. I was past that stage. There was nothing mysterious in the letter, save its conclusion. It was simply an invitation to a public meeting of the Society, which was to be held on that day week in the hall in Hanover Square, and the special feature in the letter—seeing that it did not vanish like the telegram, but remained an ordinary sheet of paper—lay in its concluding sentence. This urged me to allow nothing to prevent my attendance. " You will perhaps understand thereafter that we are neither political plotters nor lunatics, as you have thought."

Thought ! The man's mysterious power was becoming wearisome. It was too much for me. I wished that I had never seen his face.

As I lay sleepless in my bed, I recommenced that interminable introspection which, heretofore, had been so barren of result. It was easy to swear to myself that I would stand by Natalie Brande, that I would never desert her. But how should my action be directed in order that by its conduct I might prevail upon the girl herself to surrender her evil associates ? I knew that she regarded me with affection. And I knew also that she would not leave her brother for my sake. Did she sympathise with his nefarious schemes, or was she decoyed into them like myself?

Decoyed ! That was it !

I sprang from the bed, beside myself with delight. Now I had not merely a loophole of escape from all these miseries ; I had a royal highway. Fool, idiot, blind mole that I was, not to perceive sooner that easy solution of the problem! No wonder that she was wounded by my unworthy doubts. And she had tried to explain, but I would not listen! I threw myself back and commenced to weave all manner of pleasant fancies round the salvation of this girl from her brother's baneful influence, and the annihilation of his Society, despite its occult powers, by mine own valour. The reaction was too great. Instead of constructing marvellous counterplots, I fell sound asleep.

Next day I found Natalie in a pleasant morning-room to which I was directed. She wore her most extreme—and, in consequence, most exasperating—rational costume. When I entered the room she pushed a chair towards me, in a way that suggested Miss Metford's worst manner, and lit a cigarette, for the express purpose, I felt, of annoying me.

"I have come," I said somewhat shamefacedly, "to explain."

"And apologise?"

"Yes, to apologise. I made a hideous mistake. I have suffered for it as much as you could wish."

"Wish you to suffer!" She flung away her cigarette. Her dark eyes opened wide in unassumed surprise. And that curious light of pity, which I had so often wondered at, came into them. "I am very sorry if you have suffered," she said, with convincing earnestness.

"How could I doubt you? Senseless fool that I was to suppose for one moment that you approved of what you could not choose but know—"

At this her face clouded.

"I am afraid you are still in error. What opinion have you formed which alters your estimate of me?"

"The only opinion possible: that you have unwillingly learned the secret of your brother's Society; but, like myself—you see no way to— to—"

"To what purpose?"

"To destroy it."

"I am not likely to attempt that."

"No, it would be impossible, and the effort would cost your life."

"That is not my reason." She arose and stood facing me. "I do not like to lose your esteem. You know already that I will not lie to retain it. I approve of the Society's purpose."

"And its actions?"

"They are inevitable. Therefore I approve also of its actions. I shall not ask you to remain now, for I see that you are again horrified; as is natural, considering your knowledge—or, pardon me for saying so, your want of knowledge. I shall be glad to see you after the lecture to which you are invited. You will know a little more then; not all, perhaps, but enough to shake your time-dishonoured' theories of life—and death."

I bowed, and left the room without a word. It was true, then, that she was mad like the others, or worse than mad—a thousand times worse! I said farewell to Brande, as his guest, for the last time. Thenceforward I would meet him as his enemy—his secret enemy as far as I could preserve my secrecy with such a man; his open enemy when the proper time should come.

In the railway carriage I turned over some letters and papers which I found in my pockets, not with deliberate intention, but to while away the time. One scrap startled me. It was the sheet on which Brande had written the Woking address, and on reading it over once more, a thought occurred to me which I acted on as soon as possible. I could go to Woking and find out something about the man Delany. So long as my inquiries were kept within the limits of the strictest discretion, neither Brande nor any of his executive could blame me for seeking convincing evidence of the secret power they claimed.

On my arrival in London, I drove immediately to the London Necropolis Company's station and caught the funeral train which runs to Brookwood cemetery. With Saint Anne's Chapel as my base, I made short excursions hither and thither, and stood before a tombstone erected to the memory of George Delany, late of the Criminal Investigation Department, Scotland Yard. This was a clue which I could follow, so I hurried back to town and called on the superintendent of the department.

Yes, I was told, Delany had belonged to the department. He had been a very successful officer in ferreting out foreign Anarchists and evil-doers. His last movement was to join a Society of harmless cranks who met in Hanover Square. No importance was attached to this in the department. It could not have been done in the way of business, although Delany pretended that it was. He had dropped dead in the street as he was leaving his cab to enter the office with information which must have appeared to him important—to judge from the cabman's evidence as to his intense excitement and repeated directions for faster driving. There was an inquest and a post-mortem, but "death from natural causes" was the verdict. That was all. It was enough for me.

I had now sufficient evidence, and was finally convinced that the Society was as dangerous as it was demented.

CHAPTER IX.

WHEN I arrived at the Society's rooms on the evening for which I had an invitation, I found them pleasantly lighted. The various scientific diagrams and instruments had been removed, and comfortable arm-chairs were arranged so that a free passage was available, not merely to each row, but to each chair. The place was full when I entered, and soon afterwards the door was closed and locked. Natalie Brande and Edith Metford were seated beside each other. An empty chair was on Miss Metford's right. She saw me standing at the door and nodded toward the empty seat which she had reserved for me. When I reached it she made a movement as if to forestall me and leave me the middle chair. I deprecated this by a look which was intentionally so severe that she described it later as a malignant scowl.

I could not at the moment seat myself voluntarily beside Natalie Brande with the exact and final knowledge which I had learnt at Scotland Yard only one week old. I could not do it just then, although I did not mean to draw back from what I had undertaken—to stand by her, innocent or guilty. But I must have time to become accustomed to the sensation which followed this knowledge. Miss Metford's fugitive attempts at conversation pending the commencement of the lecture were disagreeable to me.

There was a little stir on the platform. The chairman, in a few words, announced Herbert Brande. "This is the first public lecture," he said, "which has been given since the formation of the Society, and in consequence of the fact that a number of people not scientifically educated are present, the lecturer will avoid the more esoteric phases of his subject, which would otherwise present themselves in his treatment of it, and confine himself to the commonplaces of scientific insight. The title of the lecture is identical with that of our Society—*Cui Bono ?*"

Brande came forward unostentatiously and placed a roll of paper on the reading-desk. I have copied the extracts which follow from this manuscript. The whole essay, indeed, remains with me

intact, but it is too long—and it would be im-
material—to reproduce it all in this narrative. I
cannot hope either to reproduce the weird impres-
siveness of the lecturer's personality, his hold over
his audience, or my own emotions in listening to
this man—whom I had proved, not only from his
own confession, but by the strongest collateral
evidence, to be a callous and relentless murderer—
to hear him glide with sonorous voice and graceful
gesture from point to point in his logical and
terrible indictment of suffering!—the futility of it,
both in itself and that by which it was administered! No one could know Brande without
finding interest, if not pleasure, in his many chance
expressions full of curious and mysterious thought.
I had often listened to his extemporaneous brain
pictures, as the reader knows, but I had never
before heard him deliberately formulate a planned-
out system of thought. And such a system! This
is the gospel according to Brande.

"In the verbiage of primitive optimism a misleading limitation is placed on the significance of
the word Nature and its inflections. And the mis-
conception of the meaning of an important word is
as certain to lead to an inaccurate concept as is the
misstatement of a premise to precede a false con-

clusion. For instance, in the aphorism, variously rendered, 'what is natural is right,' there is an excellent illustration of the misapplication of the word 'natural.' If the saying means that what is natural is just and wise, it might as well run 'what is natural is wrong,' injustice and unwisdom being as natural, *i.e.*, a part of Nature, as justice and wisdom. Morbidity and immorality are as natural as health and purity. Not more so, but not less so. That 'Nature is made better by no mean but Nature makes that mean,' is true enough. It is inevitably true. The question remains, in making that mean, has she really made anything that tends toward the final achievement of universal happiness? I say she has not.

"The misuse of a word, it may be argued, could not prove a serious obstacle to the growth of knowledge, and might be even interesting to the student of etymology. But behind the misuse of the word 'natural' there is a serious confusion of thought which must be clarified before the mass of human intelligence can arrive at a just appreciation of the verities which surround human existence, and explain it. To this end it is necessary to get rid of the archaic idea of Nature as a paternal, providential, and beneficent protector, a successor to the 'special providence,' and to know the true Nature, bond-slave as she is of her own eternal persistence of force; that sole primary principle of which all other principles are only correlatives; of which the existence of matter is but a cognisable evidence.

"The optimist notion, therefore, that Nature is an all-wise designer, in whose work order, system, wisdom, and beauty are prominent, does not fare well when placed under the microscope of scientific research.

"Order?

"There is no order in Nature. Her armies are but seething mobs of rioters, destroying everything they can lay hands on.

"System?

"She has no system, unless it be a *reductio ad absurdum*, which only blunders on the right way after fruitlessly trying every other conceivable path. She is not wise. She never fills a pail but she spills a hogshead. All her works are not beautiful. She never makes a masterpiece but she smashes a million 'wasters' without a care. The theory of evolution — her gospel—reeks with ruffianism, nature-patented and promoted. The whole scheme of the universe, all material existence as it is popularly known, is founded upon and begotten of a system of everlasting suffering as hideous as the fantastic nightmares of religious maniacs. The Spanish Inquisitors have been regarded as the most unnatural monsters who ever disgraced the history of mankind. Yet the atrocities of the Inquisitors, like the battlefields of Napoleon and other heroes, were not only natural, but they have their prototypes in every cubic inch of stagnant water, or ounce of diseased tissue. And stagnant water is as natural as sterilised water; and diseased tissue is as natural as healthy tissue. Wholesale murder is Nature's first law. She creates only to kill, and applies the rule as remorselessly to the units in a star-drift as to the tadpoles in a horse-pond.

"It seems a far cry from a star-drift to a horse-pond. It is so in distance and magnitude. It is not in the matter of constituents. In ultimate composition they are identical. The great nebula in Andromeda is an aggregation of atoms, and so is the river Thames. The only difference between them is the difference in the arrangement and incidence of these atoms and in the molecular motion of which they are the first but not the final cause. In a pint of Thames water, we know that there is bound up a latent force beside which steam and electricity are powerless in comparison. To release that force it is only necessary to apply the sympathetic key ; just as the heated point of a needle will explode a mine of gunpowder and lay a city in ashes. That force is asleep. The atoms which could give it reality are at rest, or, at least, in a condition of *quasi* rest. But in the stupendous mass of incandescent gas which constitutes the nebula of Andromeda, every atom is madly seeking rest and finding none ; whirling in raging haste, battling with every other atom in its field of motion, impinging upon others and influencing them, being impinged upon and influenced by them. That awful cauldron exemplifies admirably the method of progress stimulated by suffering. It is the embryo of a new Sun and his planets. After many million years of molecular agony, when his season of fission had come, he will rend huge fragments from his mass and hurl them helpless into space, there to grow into his satellites. In their turn they may reproduce themselves in like manner before their true planetary life begins, in which they shall revolve around their parent as solid spheres. Follow them further and learn how beneficent Nature deals with them.

"After the lapse of time-periods which man may calculate in figures, but of which his finite mind cannot form even a true symbolic conception, the outer skin of the planet cools—rests. Internal troubles prevail for longer periods still; and these, in their unsupportable agony, bend and burst the solid strata overlying; vomit fire through their self-made blow-holes, rear mountains from the depths of the sea, then dash them in pieces.

"Time strides on austere.

"The globe still cools. Life appears upon it. Then begins anew the old strife, but under conditions far more dreadful, for though it be founded on atomic consciousness, the central consciousness of the heterogeneous aggregation of atoms becomes immeasurably more sentient and susceptible with every step it takes from homogenesis. This internecine war must continue while any creature great or small shall remain alive upon the world that bore it.

"By slow degrees the mighty milestones in the protoplasmic march are passed. Plants and animals are now busy, murdering and devouring each other—the strong everywhere destroying the weak. New types appear. Old types dis-

appear. Types possessing the greatest capacity
for murder progress most rapidly, and those
with the least recede and determine. The neoli-
thic man succeeds the palæolithic man, and
sharpens the stone axe. Then to increase their
power for destruction, men find it better to hunt
in packs. Communities appear. Soon each community discovers that its own advantage is
furthered by confining its killing, in the main,
to the members of neighbouring communities.
Nations early make the same discovery. And at
last, as with ourselves, there is established a race
with conscience enough to know that it is vile,
and intelligence enough to know that it is insignificant.[1] But what profits this? In the
fulness of its time the race shall die. Man will
go down into the pit, and all his thoughts will
perish. The uneasy consciousness which, in
this obscure corner, has for a brief space broken
the silence of the Universe, will be at rest. Matter
will know itself no longer. Life and death and
love, stronger than death, will be as though they
never had been. Nor will anything that *is* be

[1] From this sentence to the end of the paragraph Brande
draws freely, for the purpose of his own argument, on Mr.
Balfour's " Naturalism and Ethics."—*Ed.*

better or be worse for all that the labour, genius, devotion, and suffering of man have striven through countless generations to effect.

"The roaring loom of Time weaves on. The globe cools out. Life mercifully ceases from upon its surface. The atmosphere and water disappear. It rests. It is dead.

"But for its vicarious service in influencing more youthful planets within its reach, that dead world might as well be loosed at once from its gravitation cable and be turned adrift into space. Its time has not yet come. It will not come until the great central sun of the system to which it belongs has passed laboriously through all his stages of stellar life and died out also. Then when that dead sun, according to the impact theory, blunders across the path of another sun, dead and blind like himself, its time will come. The result of that impact will be a new star nebula, with all its weary history before it; a history of suffering, in which a million years will not be long enough to write a single page.

"Here we have a scientific parallel to the hell of superstition which may account for the instinctive origin of the smoking flax and the fire which shall never be quenched. We know that the atoms of which the human body is built up are atoms of matter. It follows that every atom in every living body will be present in some form at that final impact in which the solar system will be ended in a blazing whirlwind which will melt the earth with its fervent heat. There is not a molecule or cell in any creature alive this day which will not in its ultimate constituents endure the long agony, lasting countless æons of centuries, wherein the solid mass of this great globe will be represented by a rush of incandescent gas, stupendous in itself, but trivial in comparison with the hurricane of flame in which it will be swallowed up and lost.

"And when from that hell a new star emerges, and new planets in their season are born of him, and he and they repeat, as they must repeat, the ceaseless, changeless, remorseless story of the universe, every atom in this earth will take its place, and fill again functions identical with those which it, or its fellow, fills now. Life will reappear, develop, determine, to be renewed again as before. And so on for ever.

"Nature has known no rest. From the beginning—which never was—she has been building up only to tear down again. She has been fabricating pretty toys and trinkets, that cost her many a thousand years to forge, only to break them in pieces for her sport. With infinite painstaking she has manufactured man only to torture him with mean miseries in the embryonic stages of his race, and in his higher development to madden him with intellectual puzzles. Thus it will be unto the end—which never shall be. For there is neither beginning nor end to her unvarying cycles. Whether the secular optimist be successful or unsuccessful in realising his paltry span of terrestrial paradise, whether the pæans he sings about it are prophetic dithyrambs or misleading myths, no Christian man need fear for his own immortality. That is well assured. In some form he will surely be raised from the dead. In some shape he will live again. But, *Cui bono?*"

CHAPTER X.

FORCE—A REMEDY.

"GET me out of this, I am stifled—ill," Miss Metford said, in a low voice to me.

As we were hurrying from the room, Brande and his sister, who had joined him, met us. The fire had died out of his eyes. His voice had returned to its ordinary key. His demeanour was imperturable, sphinx-like. I murmured some words about the eloquence of the lecture, but interrupted myself when I observed his complete indifference to my remarks, and said,

"Neither praise nor blame seems to affect you, Brande."

"Certainly not," he answered calmly. "You forget that there is nothing deserving of either praise or blame."

I knew I could not argue with him, so we passed on. Outside, I offered to find a cab for Miss Metford, and to my surprise she allowed

me to do so. Her self-assertive manner was
visibly modified. She made no pretence of re-
senting this slight attention, as was usual with
her in similar cases. Indeed, she asked me to
accompany her as far as our ways lay together.
But I felt that my society at the time could
hardly prove enlivening. I excused myself by
saying candidly that I wished to be alone.

My own company soon became unendurable.
In despair I turned into a music hall. The
contrast between my mental excitement and the
inanities of the stage was too acute, so this
resource speedily failed me. Then I betook
myself to the streets again. Here I remembered a letter Brande had put into my hand
as I left the hall. It was short, and the tone
was even more peremptory than his usual
arrogance. It directed me to meet the members
of the Society at Charing Cross station at two
o'clock on the following day. No information
was given, save that we were all going on a
long journey; that I must set my affairs in
such order that my absence would not cause
any trouble, and the letter ended, "Our experiments are now complete. Our plans are
matured. Do not fail to attend."

"Fail to attend!" I muttered. "If I am not the most abject coward on the earth I will attend—with every available policeman in London." The pent-up wrath and impotence of many days found voice at last. "Yes, Brande," I shouted aloud, "I will attend, and you shall be sorry for having invited me."

"But I will not be sorry," said Natalie Brande, touching my arm.

"You here!" I exclaimed, in great surprise, for it was fully an hour since I left the hall, and my movements had been at haphazard since then.

"Yes, I have followed you for your own sake. Are you really going to draw back now?"

"I must."

"Then I must go on alone."

"You will not go on alone. You will remain, and your friends shall go on without you— go to prison without you, I mean."

"Poor boy," she said softly, to herself. "I wonder if I would have thought as I think now if I had known him sooner? I suppose I should have been as other women, and their fools' paradise would have been mine—for a little while."

The absolute hopelessness in her voice pierced my heart. I pleaded passionately with her to give up her brother and all the maniacs who followed him. For the time I forgot utterly that the girl, by her own confession, was already with them in sympathy as well as in deed.

She said to me: "I cannot hold back now. And you? You know you are powerless to interfere. If you will not come with me, I must go alone. But you may remain. I have prevailed on Herbert and Grey to permit that."

"Never," I answered. "Where you go, I go."

"It is not really necessary. In the end it will make no difference. And remember, you still think me guilty."

"Even so, I am going with you—guilty."

Now this seemed to me a very ordinary speech, for who would have held back, thinking her innocent? But Natalie stopped suddenly, and, looking me in the face, said, almost with a sob:

"Arthur, I sometimes wish I had known you sooner. I might have been different." She was silent for a moment. Then she said piteously to me: "You will not fail me to-morrow?"

"No, I will not fail you to-morrow," I answered.

She pressed my hand gratefully, and left me without any explanation as to her movements in the meantime.

I hurried to my hotel to set my affairs in order before joining Brande's expedition. The time was short for this. Fortunately there was not much to do. By midnight I had my arrangements nearly complete. At the time, the greater part of my money was lying at call in a London bank. This I determined to draw in gold the next day. I also had at my banker's some scrip, and I knew I could raise money on that. My personal effects and the mementos of my travels, which lay about my rooms in great confusion, must remain where they were. As to the few friends who still remained to me, I did not write to them. I could not well describe a project of which I knew nothing, save that it was being carried out by dangerous lunatics, or, at least, by men who were dangerous, whether their madness was real or assumed. Nor could I think of any reasonable excuse for leaving England after so long an absence without a personal visit to them. It was best, then, to disappear without a word. Having finished my dispositions, I changed my coat for a dressing-gown and sat down by the window, which

G

I threw open, for the summer night was warm.   I
sat long, and did not leave my chair until the
morning sun was shining on my face.

When I got to Charing Cross next day, a group
of fifty or sixty people were standing apart from
the general crowd and conversing with animation.
Almost the whole strength of the Society was
assembled to see a few of us off, I thought.   In
fact, they were all going.   About a dozen women
were in the party, and they were dressed in the
most extravagant rational costumes.   Edith Metford was amongst them.   I drew her aside, and
apologised for not having called to wish her farewell ; but she stopped me.

"Oh, it's all right ; I am going too.   Don't look
so frightened."

This was more than I could tolerate.   She was
far too good a girl to be allowed to walk blindfold
into the pit I had digged for myself with full
knowledge.   I said imperatively :

"Miss Metford, you shall not go.   I warned you
more than once—and warned you, I firmly believe,
at the risk of my life—against these people.   You
have disregarded the advice which it may yet
cost me dear to have given you."

"To tell you the truth," she said candidly, " I

would not go an inch if it were not for yourself.
I can't trust you with them. You'd get into mischief. I don't mean with Natalie Brande, but the
others; I don't like them. So I am coming to
look after you."

" Then I shall speak to Brande."

" That would be useless. I joined the Society
this morning."

This she said seriously, and without anything
of the spirit of bravado which was one of her
faults. That ended our dispute. We exchanged a
meaning look as our party took their seats. There
was now, at any rate, one human being in the
Society to whom I could speak my mind.

We travelled by special train. Our ultimate
destination was a fishing village on the southern
coast, near Brande's residence. Here we found a
steam yacht of about a thousand tons lying in the
harbour with steam up. .

The vessel was a beautiful model. Her lines
promised great speed, but the comfort of her passengers had been no less considered by her builder
when he gave her so much beam and so high
a freeboard. The ship's furniture was the finest
I had ever seen, and I had crossed every great
ocean in the world. The library, especially, was

more suggestive of a room in the British Museum
than the batch of books usually carried at sea.
But I have no mind to enter on a detailed description of a beautiful pleasure ship while my
story waits. I only mention the general condition of the vessel in evidence of the fact which
now struck me for the first time—Brande must
have unlimited money. His mode of life in
London and in the country, notwithstanding his
pleasant house, was in the simplest style. From
the moment we entered his special train at
Charing Cross, he flung money about him with
wanton recklessness.

As we made our way through the crowd which
was hanging about the quay, an unpleasant incident occurred. Miss Brande, with Halley and
Rockingham, became separated from Miss Metford and myself and went on in front of us. We
five had formed a sub-section of the main body,
and were keeping to ourselves when the unavoid-
able separation took place. A slight scream in
front caused Miss Metford and myself to hurry
forward. We found the others surrounded by a
gang of drunken sailors, who had stopped them.
A red-bearded giant, frenzied with drink, had
seized Natalie in his arms. His abettor, a

swarthy Italian, had drawn his knife, and men-
aced Halley and Rockingham. The rest of the
band looked on, and cheered their chiefs. Halley
was white to the lips; Rockingham was perfectly
calm, or, perhaps, indifferent. He called for a
policeman. Neither interfered. I did not blame
Rockingham; he was a man of the world, so
nothing manly could be expected of him. But
Halley's cowardice disgusted me.

I rushed forward and caught the Italian from
behind, for his knife was dangerous. Seizing
him by the collar and waist, I swung him twice,
and then flung him from me with all my strength.
He spun round two or three times, and then
collided with a stack of timber. His head struck
a beam, and he fell in his tracks without a word.
The red-haired giant instantly released Natalie
and put up his hands. The man's attitude
showed that he knew nothing of defence. I
swept his guard aside, and struck him violently
on the neck close to the ear. I was a trained
boxer; but I had never before struck a blow in
earnest, or in such earnest, and I hardly knew
my own strength. The man went down with a
grunt like a pole-axed ox, and lay where he fell.
To a drunken sailor lad, who seemed anxious to

be included in this matter, I dealt a stinging smack on the face with my open hand that satisfied him straightway. The others did not molest me. Turning from the crowd, I found Edith Metford looking at me with blazing eyes.

"Superb! Marcel, I am proud of you!" she cried.

"Oh! Edith, how can you say that?" Natalie Brande exclaimed, still trembling. "Such dreadful violence! The poor men knew no better."

"Poor fiddlesticks! It is well for you that Marcel is a man of violence. He's worth a dozen sheep like—"

"Like whom, Miss Metford?" Rockingham asked, glaring at her so viciously that I interposed with a hasty entreaty that all should hurry to the ship. I did not trust the man.

Miss Metford was not so easily suppressed. She said leisurely, "I meant to say like you, and this over-nervous but otherwise admirable boy. If you think 'sheep' derogatory, pray make it 'goats.'"

I hurried them on board. Brande welcomed us at the gangway. The vessel was his own, so he was as much at home on the ship as in his country house. I had an important letter to write,

and very little time for the task. It was not
finished a moment too soon, for the moment the
last passenger and the last bale of luggage was
on board, the captain's telegraph rang from the
bridge, and the *Esmeralda* steamed out to sea.
My letter, however, was safe on shore. The land
was low down upon the horizon before the long
summer twilight deepened slowly into night.
Then one by one the shadowy cliffs grew dim,
dark, and disappeared. We saw no more of
England until after many days of gradually culminating horror. The very night which was our
first at sea did not pass without a strange adventure, which happened, indeed, by an innocent
oversight.

CHAPTER XI.

MORITURI TE SALUTANT.

WE had been sitting on deck chairs smoking and talking for a couple of hours after the late dinner, which was served as soon as the vessel was well out to sea, when Brande came on deck. He was hailed with enthusiasm. This did not move him, or even interest him. I was careful not to join in the acclamations produced by his presence. He noticed this, and lightly called me recalcitrant. I admitted the justice of the epithet, and begged him to consider it one which would always apply to me with equal force. He laughed at this, and contrasted my gloomy fears with the excellent arrangements which he had made for my comfort. I asked him what had become of Grey. I thought it strange that this man should be amongst the absentees.

"Oh, Grey! He goes to Labrador."

"To Labrador! What takes him to Labrador?"

"The same purpose which takes us to the Arafura Sea," Brande answered, and passed on.

Presently there was a slight stir amongst the people, and the word was passed round that Brande was about to undertake some interesting experiment for the amusement of his guests. I hurried aft along with some other men with whom I had been talking, and found Miss Brande and Miss Metford standing hand in hand. Natalie's face was very white, and the only time I ever saw real fear upon it was at that moment. I thought the incident on the quay had unnerved her more than was apparent at the time, and that she was still upset by it. She beckoned to me, and when I came to her she seized my hand. She was trembling so much her words were hardly articulate. Miss Metford was concerned for her companion's nervousness; but otherwise indifferent; while Natalie stood holding our hands in hers like a frightened child awaiting the firing of a cannon.

"He's going to let off something, a rocket, I suppose," Miss Metford said to me. "Natalie seems to think he means to sink the ship."

"He does not mean to do so. He might, if an accident occurred."

"Is he going to fire a mine?" I asked.

"No, he is going to etherize a drop of water." Natalie said this so seriously, we had no thought of laughter, incongruous as the cause of her fears might seem.

At that moment Brande addressed us from the top of the deckhouse, and explained that, in order to illustrate on a large scale the most recent discovery in natural science, he was about to disintegrate a drop of water, at present encased in a hollow glass ball about the size of a pea, which he held between his thumb and forefinger. An electric light was turned upon him so that we could all see the thing quite plainly. He explained that there was a division in the ball; one portion of it containing the drop of water, and the other the agent by which, when the dividing wall was eaten through by its action, the atoms of the water would be resolved into the ultimate ether of which they were composed. As the disintegrating agent was powerless in salt water, we might all feel assured that no great catastrophe would ensue.

Before throwing the glass ball overboard, a

careful search for the lights of ships was made from east to west, and north to south.

There was not a light to be seen anywhere. Brande threw the ball over the side. We were going under easy steam at the time, but the moment he left the deckhouse "full speed ahead" was rung from the bridge, and the *Esmeralda* showed us her pace. She literally tore through the water when the engines were got full on.

Before we had gone a hundred yards a great cry arose. A little fleet of French fishing-boats with no lights up had been lying very close to us on the starboard bow. There they were, boatfuls of men, who waved careless adieus to us as we dashed past.

Brande was moved for a moment. Then he shrugged his shoulders and muttered, "It can't be helped now." We all felt that these simple words might mean much. To test their full portent I went over to him, Natalie still holding my hand with trembling fingers.

" Can't you do anything for them ? " I asked.

" You mean, go back and sink this ship to keep them company ? "

" No ; but warn them to fly."

" It would be useless. In this breeze they could

not sail a hundred yards in the time allowed, and three miles is the nearest point of safety. I could not say definitely, as this is the first time I have ever tried an experiment so tremendous; but I believe that if we even slowed to half speed, it would be dangerous, and if we stopped, the *Esmeralda* would go to the bottom to-night, as certainly as the sun will rise to-morrow."

Natalie moaned in anguish on hearing this. I said to her sternly:

"I thought you approved of all these actions?"

"This serves no purpose. These men may not even have a painless death, and the reality is more awful than I thought."

Every face was turned to that point in the darkness toward which the foaming wake of the *Esmeralda* stretched back. Not a word more was spoken until Brande, who was standing, watch in hand, beside the light from the deckhouse, came aft and said:

"You will see the explosion in ten seconds."

He could not have spoken more indifferently if the catastrophe he had planned was only the firing of a penny squib.

Then the sea behind us burst into a flame, followed by the sound of an explosion so frightful that we were almost stunned by it. A huge mass of water, torn up in a solid block, was hurled into the air, and there it broke into a hundred roaring cataracts. These, in the brilliant search light from the ship which was now turned upon them full, fell like cataracts of liquid silver into the seething cauldron of water that raged below. The instant the explosion was over, our engines were reversed, and the *Esmeralda* went full speed astern. The waves were still rolling in tumultuous breakers when we got back. We might as well have gone on.

The French fishing fleet had disappeared.

I could not help saying to Brande before we turned in :

"You expect us, I suppose, to believe that the explosion was really caused by a drop of water ? "

" Etherized," he interrupted. " Certainly I do. You don't believe it—on what grounds ? "

" That it is unbelievable."

" Pshaw ! You deny a fact because you do not understand it. Ignorance is not evidence."

" I say it is impossible."

" You do not wish to believe it possible. Wishes are not proofs."

Without pursuing the argument, I said to him :

"It is fortunate that the accident took place at sea. There will be no inquests."

"Oh! I am sorry for the accident. As for the men, they might have had a worse fate. It is better than living in life-long misery as they do. Besides, both they and the fishes that will eat them will soon be numbered amongst the things that have been."

CHAPTER XII.

FOR some days afterwards our voyage was un-eventful, and the usual ship-board amusements were requisitioned to while away the tedious hours. The French fishing fleet was never men-tioned. We got through the Bay with very little knocking about, and passed the Rock without calling. I was not disappointed, for there was slight inducement for going ashore, oppressed as I was with the ever-present incubus of dread. At intervals this feeling became less acute, but only to return, strengthened by its short absences. After a time my danger sense became blunted. The nervous system became torpid under continu-ous stress, and refused to pass on the sensations with sufficient intensity to the brain; or the weary brain was asleep at its post and did not heed the warnings. I could think no more.

And this reminds me of something which I must

tell about young Halley.   For several days after
the voyage began, the boy avoided me.   I knew
his reason for doing this.   I myself did not blame
him for his want of physical courage, but I was
glad that he himself was ashamed of it.

Halley came to me one morning and said :

"I wish to speak to you, Marcel.   I *must*
speak to you.   It is about that miserable episode
on the evening we left England.   I acted like a
cad.   Therefore I must be a cad.   I only want to
tell you that I despise myself as much as you can.
And that I envy you.   I never thought that I
should envy a man simply because he had no
nervous system."

"Who is this man without a nervous system of
whom you speak ? " I asked coldly.   I was not
sorry that I had an opportunity of reading him a
lesson which might be placed opposite the many
indignities which had been put upon me, in the
form mainly of shoulder shrugs, brow elevations,
and the like.

"You, of course.   I mean no offence—you are
magnificent.   I am honest in saying that I admire
you.   I wish I was like you in height, weight,
muscle—and absence of nervous system."

"You would keep your own brain, I suppose?" I asked.

"Yes, I would keep that."

"And I will keep my own nervous system," I replied. "And the difference between mine and yours is this: that whereas my own danger sense is, or was, as keen as your own, I have my reserve of nerve force—or had it—which might be relied on to tide me over a sudden emergency. This reserve you have expended on your brain. There are two kinds of cowards; the selfish coward who cares for no interest save his own; the unselfish coward who cares nothing for himself, but who cannot face a danger because he dare not. And there are two kinds of brave men; the nerveless man you spoke of, who simply faces danger because he does not appreciate it, and the man who faces danger because, although he fears it he dares it. I have no difficulty in placing you in this list."

"You place me—"

"A coward because you cannot help it. You are merely out of harmony with your environment. You ought to bring a supply of 'environment' about with you, seeing that you cannot manufacture it off-hand like myself. I wish to be alone. Good-day."

H

"Before I go, Marcel, I will say this." There were tears in his eyes. "These people do not really know you, with all their telepathic power. You are not—not—"

"Not as great a fool as they think. Thank you. I mean to prove that to them some day."

With that I turned away from him, although I felt that he would have gladly stayed longer with me.

While the *Esmeralda* was sweeping over the long swells of the Mediterranean, I heard Brande lecture for the second time. It was a fitting interlude between his first and third addresses. I might classify them thus—the first, critical; the second, constructive; the third, executive. His third speech was the last he made in the world.

We were assembled in the saloon. It would have been pleasanter on the upper deck, owing to the heat, but the speaker could not then have been easily heard in the noise of the wind and waves. I could scarcely believe that it was Brande who arose to speak, so changed was his expression. The frank scepticism, which had only recently degenerated into a cynicism, still tempered with a half kindly air of easy superiority, was gone.

In its place there was a look of concentrated and relentless purpose which dominated the man himself and all who saw him. He began in forcible and direct sentences, with only a faintly reminiscent eloquence which was part of himself, and from which he could not without a conscious effort have freed his style. But the whole bearing of the man had little trace in it of the dilettante academician whom we all remembered.

" When I last addressed this Society," he began, " I laboured under a difficulty in arriving at ultimate truth which was of my own manufacture. I presupposed, as you will remember, the indestructibility of the atom, and, in logical consequence I was bound to admit the conservation of suffering, the eternity of misery. But on that evening many of my audience were untaught in the rudiments of ultimate thought, and some were still sceptical of the *bona fides* of our purpose, and our power to achieve its object. To them, in their then ineptitude, what I shall say now would have been unintelligible. For in the same way that the waves of light or sound exceeding a certain maximum can not be transferred to the brain by dull eyes and ears, my thought pulsations would have escaped those auditors by virtue of their own irresponsiveness. To-night I am free from the limitation which I then suffered, because there are none around me now who have not sufficient knowledge to grasp what I shall present.

"You remember that I traced for you the story of evolution in its journey from the atom to the star. And I showed you that the hypothesis of the indestructibility of the atom was simply a creed of cruelty writ large. I now proceed on the lines of true science to show you how that hypothesis is false; that as the atom *is* destructible—as you have seen by our experiments (the last of which resulted in a climax not intended by me)—the whole scheme of what is called creation falls to pieces. As the atom was the first etheric blunder, so the material Universe is the grand · etheric mistake.

"In considering the marvellous and miserable succession of errors resulting from the meretricious atomic remedy adopted by the ether to cure its local sores, it must first be said of the ether itself that there is too much of it. Space is not sufficient for it. Thus, the particles of ether—those imponderable entities which vibrate through a block of marble or a disc of hammered steel with only a dulled, not an annihilated motion, are by their

own tumultuous plenty packed closer together
than they wish. I say wish, for if all material
consciousness and sentiency be founded on atomic
consciousness, then in its turn atomic consciousness
is founded upon, and dependent on, etheric consciousness. These particles of ether, therefore,
when too closely impinged upon by their neigh-
bours, resent the impact, and in doing so initiate
etheric whirlwinds, from whose vast perturbances
stupendous drifts set out. In their gigantic power
these avalanches crush the particles which impede ✔
them, force the resisting medium out of its normal
stage, destroy the homogeneity of its constituents,
and mass them into individualistic communities
whose vibrations play with greater freedom when
they synchronise. The homogeneous etheric
tendencies recede and finally determine.

" Behold a miracle! An atom is born!

" By a similar process—which I may liken to
that of putting off an evil day which some time
must be endured—the atoms group themselves into
molecules. In their turn the molecules go forth to
war, capturing or being captured; the vibrations
of the slaves always being forced to synchronise
with those of their conquerors. The nucleus of
the gas of a primal metal is now complete, and the

foundation of a solar system—paltry molecule of the Universe as it is—is laid. Thereafter, the rest is easily followed. It is described in your school books, and must not occupy me now.

"But one word I will interpolate which may serve to explain a curious and interesting human belief. You are aware of how, in times past, men of absolutely no scientific insight held firmly to the idea that an elixir of life and a philosopher's stone might be discovered, and that these two objects were nearly always pursued contemporaneously. That is to my mind an extraordinary example of the force of atomic consciousness. The idea itself was absolutely correct; but the men who followed it had slight knowledge of its unity, and none whatever of its proper pursuit. They would have worked on their special lines to eternity before advancing a single step toward their object. And this because they did not know what life was, and death was, and what the metals ultimately signified which they, blind fools, so unsuccessfully tried to transmute. But we know more than they. We have climbed no doubt in the footholds they have carved, and we have gained the summit they only saw in the mirage of hope. For we know that there is no life, no death, no metals, no matter, no emotions, no thoughts; but that all that we call by these names is only the ether in various conditions. Life! I could live as long as this earth will submit to human existence if I had studied that paltry problem. Metals! The ship in which you sail was bought with gold manufactured in my crucibles.

"The unintelligent—or I should say the grossly ignorant—have long held over the heads of the pioneers of science these two great charges: No man has ever yet transmuted a metal; no man has ever yet proved the connecting link between organic and inorganic life. I say *life*, for I take it that this company admits that a slab of granite is as much alive as any man or woman I see before me. But I have manufactured gold, and I could have manufactured protoplasm if I had devoted my life to that object. My studies have been almost wholly on the inorganic plane. Hence the 'philosopher's stone' came in my way, but not the 'elixir of life.' The molecules of protoplasm are only a little more complex than the molecules of hydrogen or nitrogen or iron or coal. You may fuse iron, vaporise water, intermix the gases; but the molecules of all change little in such metamorphosis. And you may slay twenty thousand men at Waterloo or Sedan, or ten thousand generations may be numbered with the dust, and not an ounce of protoplasm lies dead. All molecules are merely arrangements of atoms made under different degrees of pressure and of different ages. And all atoms are constructed of identical constituents—the ether, as I have said. Therefore the ether, which was from the beginning, is now, and ever shall be, which is the same yesterday, to-day, and for ever, is the origin of force, of matter, of life.

" *It is alive !*

" Its starry children are so many that the sands of the seashore may not be used as a similitude for their multitude ; and they extend so far that distance may not be named in relation to them. They are so high above us and so deep below us that there is neither height nor depth in them. There is neither east nor west in them, nor north and south in them. Nor is there beginning or end to them. Time drops his scythe and stands appalled before that dreadful host. Number applies not to its eternal multitudes. Distance is lost in boundless space. And from all the stars that stud the caverns of the Universe, there swells this awful chorus: Failure! failure and futility! And the ether is to blame!

"Heterogeneous suffering is more acute than homogeneous, because the agony is intensified by being localised; because the comfort of the comfortable is purchasable only by the multiplied misery of the miserable; because aristocratic leisure requires that the poor should be always with it. There is, therefore, no gladness without its overbalancing sorrow. There is no good without intenser evil. There is no death save in life.

"Back, then, from this ill-balanced and unfair long-suffering, this insufficient existence. Back to Nirvana—the ether! And I will lead the way.

"The agent I will employ has cost me all life to discover. It will release the vast stores of etheric energy locked up in the huge atomic warehouse of this planet. I shall remedy the grand mistake only to a degree which it would be preposterous to call even microscopic; but when I have done what I can, I am blameless for the rest. In due season the whole blunder will be cured by the same means that I shall use, and all the hideous experiment will be over, and everlasting rest or *quasi*-rest will supersede the magnificent failure of material existence. This earth, at least, and, I am encouraged to hope, the whole solar system, will by my instrumentality be restored to the ether from which it never should have emerged. Once before, in the history of our system, an effort similar to mine was made, unhappily without success.

"This time we shall not fail!"

A low murmur rose from the audience as the lecturer concluded, and a hushed whisper asked:

"Where was that other effort made?"

Brande faced round momentarily, and said quietly but distinctly:

"On the planet which was where the Asteroids are now."

CHAPTER XIII.

WE coaled at Port Said like any ordinary steamer. Although I had more than once made the Red Sea voyage, I had never before taken the slightest interest in the coaling of the vessel on which I was a passenger. This time every-thing was different. That which interested me before seemed trivial now. And that which had before seemed trivial was now absorbing. I watched the coaling—commonplace as the spec-tacle was—with vivid curiosity. The red lights, the sooty demons at work, every bag of coals they carried, and all the coal dust clouds they created, were fitting episodes in a voyage such as ours. We took an enormous quantity of coal on board. I remained up most of the night in a frame of mind which I thought none might envy. I myself would have made light of it had I known what was still in store for the

123

Esmeralda and her company. It was nearly morning when I turned in. When I awoke we were nearing the Red Sea.

On deck, the conversation of our party was always eccentric, but this must be said for it: there was sometimes a scintillating brilliance in it that almost blinded one to its extreme absurdity. The show of high spirits which was very general was, in the main, unaffected. For the rest it was plainly assumed. But those who assumed their parts did so with a histrionic power which was all the more surprising when it is remembered that the origin of their excellent playing was centred in their own fears. I preserved a neutral attitude. I did not venture on any overt act of insubordination. That would have only meant my destruction. without any counter-balancing advantage in the way of baulking an enterprise in which I was a most unwilling participator. And to pretend what I did not feel was a task which I had neither stomach to undertake nor ability to carry out successfully. In consequence I kept my own counsel—and that of Edith Metford.

Brande was the most easily approached maniac I had ever met. His affability continued absolutely consistent. I took advantage of this to say to him on a convenient opportunity: "Why did you bring these people with you? They must all be useless, and many of them little better than a nuisance!"

"Marcel, you are improving. Have you attained the telepathic power? You have read my mind." This was said with a pleasant smile.

"I can not read your mind," I answered; "I only diagnose."

"Your diagnosis is correct. I answer you in a sentence. They are all sympathetic, and human sympathy is necessary to me until my purpose is fulfilled."

"You do not look to me for any measure of this sympathy, I trust?"

"I do not. You are antipathetic."

"I am."

"But necessary, all the same."

"So be it, until the proper time shall come."

"It will never come," Brande said firmly.

"We shall see," I replied as firmly as himself.

Next evening as we were steaming down the blue waters—deep blue they always seemed

to me — of the Red Sea, I was sitting on the
foredeck smoking and trying to think. I did
not notice how the time passed. What seemed
to me an hour at most, must have been three
or four. With the exception of the men of
the crew who were on duty, I was alone, for
the heat was intense, and most of our people
were lying in their cabins prostrated in spite
of the wind-sails which were spread from every
port to catch the breeze. My meditations were
as usual gloomy and despondent. They were
interrupted by Miss Metford. She joined me
so noiselessly that I was not aware of her presence
until she laid her hand on my arm. I started
at her touch, but she whispered a sharp warning,
so full of suppressed emotion that I instantly
recovered a semblance of unconcern.

The girl was very white and nervous. This
contrast from her usual equanimity was disquiet-
ing. She clung to me hysterically as she
gasped :

"Marcel, it is a mercy I have found you alone,
and that there is one sane man in this shipful
of lunatics."

"I am afraid you are not altogether right," I
said, as I placed a seat for her close to mine.

"I can hardly be sane when I am a voluntary passenger on board this vessel."

"Do you really think they mean what they say?" she asked hurriedly, without noticing my remark.

"I really think they have discovered the secret of extraordinary natural forces, so powerful and so terrible that no one can say what they may or may not accomplish. And that is the reason I begged you not to come on this voyage."

"What was the good of asking me not to come without giving me some reason?"

"Had I done so, they might have killed you as they have done others before."

"You might have chanced that, seeing that it will probably end that way."

"And they would certainly have killed me."

"Ah!"

I wondered at the sudden intensity of the girl's sharp gasp when I said this, and marvelled too, how she, who had always been so mannish, nestled close to me and allowed her head to sink down on my shoulder. I pitied the strong-willed, self-reliant nature which had given way under some strain of which I had yet to be told. So I stooped and touched her cheek with my lips

in a friendly way, at which she looked up to me
with half-closed eyes, and whispered in a voice
strangely soft and womanish for her:

"If they must kill us, I wish they would kill
us now."

I stroked her soft cheek gently, and urged a
less hopeless view. "Even if the worst come,
we may as well live as long as we can."

Whereupon to my surprise she, having shot
one quick glance into my eyes, put my arm away
and drew her chair apart from mine. Her head
was turned away from me, but I could not but
notice that her bosom rose and fell swiftly.
Presently she faced round again, lit a cigarette,
put her hands in the pocket of her jacket, and
her feet on another chair, and said indifferently:

"You are right. Even if the worst must come,
we may as well live as long as we can."

This sudden change in her manner surprised
me. I knew I had no art in dealing with women,
so I let it pass without comment, and looked out
at the glassy sea.

After some minutes of silence, the girl spoke
to me again.

"Do you know anything of the actual plans
of these maniacs?"

"No. I only know their preposterous purpose."

"Well, I know how it is to be done. Natalie was restless last night—you know that we share the same cabin—and she raved a bit. I kept her in her berth by sheer force, but I allowed her to talk."

This was serious. I drew my chair close to Miss Metford's and whispered, "For heaven's sake, speak low." Then I remembered Brande's power, and wrung my hands in helpless impotence. "You forget Brande. At this moment he is taking down every word we say."

"He's doing nothing of the sort."

"But you forget—"

"I don't forget. By accident I put morphia in the tonic he takes, and he is now past telepathy for some hours at least. He's sound asleep. I suppose if I had not done it by accident he would have known what I was doing, and so have refused the medicine. Anyhow, accident or no accident, I have done it."

"Thank God!" I cried.

"And this precious disintegrating agent! They haven't it with them, it seems. To manufacture it in sufficient quantity would be impossible in

I

any civilised country without fear of detection or interruption. Brande has the prescription, formula—what do you call it?—and if you could get the paper and—"

" Throw it overboard ! "

" Rubbish ! They would work it all out again."

" What then ? " I whispered.

" Steal the paper and—wouldn't it do to put in an extra x or y, or stick a couple of additional figures into any suitable vacancy ? Don't you think they'd go on with the scheme and—"

" And ? "

" And make a mess of it ! "

" Miss Metford," I said, rising from my chair, " I mean Metford, I know you like to be addressed as a man—or used to like it."

" Yes, I used to," she assented coldly.

" I am going to take you in my arms and kiss you."

" I'm hanged if you are ! " she exclaimed, so sharply that I was suddenly abashed. My intended familiarity and its expression appeared grotesque, although a few minutes before she was so friendly. But I could not waste precious time in studying a girl's caprices, so I asked at once :

" How can I get this paper ? "

" I said *steal* it, if you recollect." Her voice was now hard, almost harsh. " You can get it in Brande's cabin, if you are neither afraid nor jealous."

" I am not much afraid, and I will try it. What do you mean by jealous ? "

" I mean, would you, to save Natalie Brande— for they will certainly succeed in blowing themselves up, if nobody else—consent to her marrying another man, say that young lunatic Halley, who is always dangling after her when you are not ? "

" Yes," I answered, after some thought. For Halley's attentions to Natalie had been so marked, the plainly inconsequent mention of him in this matter did not strike me. " If that is necessary to save her, of course I would consent to it. Why do you ask ? In my place you would do the same."

" No. I'd see the ship and all its precious passengers at the bottom of the sea first."

" Ah ! but you are not a man."

"Right! and what's more, I'm glad of it." Then looking down at the rational part of her costume, she added sharply, "I sha'n't wear these things again."

CHAPTER XIV.

AT one o'clock in the morning I arose, dressed
hurriedly, drew on a pair of felt slippers, and
put a revolver in my pocket. It was then time
to put Edith Metford's proposal to the proof, and
she would be waiting for me on deck to hear
whether I had succeeded in it. We had parted
a couple of hours before on somewhat chilling
terms. I had agreed to follow her suggestion,
but I could not trouble my tired brain by guesses
at the cause of her moods.

It was very dark. There was only enough
light to enable me to find my way along the
corridor, off which the state-rooms occupied by
Brande and his immediate lieutenants opened.
All the sleepers were restless from the terrible
heat. As I stole along, a muffled word, a sigh, or
a movement in the berths, made me pause at

133

every step with a beating heart. Having listened
till all was quiet, I moved on again noiselessly.
I was almost at the end of the corridor. So in-
tent had I been on preserving perfect silence, it
did not sooner occur to me that I was searching
for any special door. I had forgotten Brande's
number !

I could no more think of it than one can recall
the name of a half-forgotten acquaintance suddenly encountered in the street. It might have
been fourteen, or forty-one, or a hundred and
fifty. Every number was as likely as it was unlikely. I tried vainly to concentrate my mind.
The result was nothing. The missing number
gave no clue. To enter the wrong room in that
ship at that hour meant death for me. Of that
I was certain. To leave the right room unentered
gave away my first chance in the unequal battle
with Brande. Then, as I knew that my first
chance would probably be my last, if not availed
of, I turned to the nearest door and quietly tried
the handle. The door was not locked. I entered
the state-room.

"What do you want?" It was Halley's voice
that came from the berth.

"Pardon me," I whispered, "a mistake. The

heat, you know. Went on deck, and have blundered into your room."

"Oh, all right. Who are you?"

"Brande."

"Good-night. You did not blunder far;" this sleepily.

I went out and closed the door quietly. I had gained something. I was within one door of my destination, for I knew that Halley was berthed between Rockingham and Brande. But I did not know on which side Brande's room was, and I dared not ask. I tried the next door going forward. It opened like the other. I went in.

"Hallo there!" This time no sleepy or careless man challenged me. It was Rockingham's voice.

"May I not enter my own room?" I whispered.

"This is not your room. You are?" Rockingham sprang up in his berth, but before he could leave it I was upon him.

"I am Arthur Marcel. And this iron ring which I press against your left ear is the muzzle of my revolver. Speak, move, breathe above your natural breath and your brains go through that porthole. Now, loose your hold of my arm and come with me."

"You fool!" hissed Rockingham. "You dare not fire. You know you dare not."

He was about to call out, but my left hand closed on his throat, and a gurgling gasp was all that issued from him.

I laid down the revolver and turned the ear of the strangling man close to my mouth. I had little time to think; but thought flies fast when such deadly peril menaces the thinker as that which I must face if I failed to make terms with the man who was in my power. I knew that notwithstanding his intensely disagreeable nature, if he gave his promise either by spoken word or equivalent sign, I could depend upon him. There were no liars in Brande's Society. But the word I could not trust him to say. I must have his sign. I whispered:

"You know I do not wish to kill you. I shall never have another happy day if you force me to it. I have no choice. You must yield or die. If you will yield and stand by me rather than against me in what shall follow, choose life by taking your right hand from my wrist and touching my left shoulder. I will not hurt you meanwhile. If you choose death, touch me with your left."

The sweat stood on my forehead in big beads as

I waited for his choice. It was soon made. He unlocked his left hand and placed it firmly on my right shoulder.

He had chosen death.

So the man was only a physical coward—or perhaps he had only made a choice of alternatives.

I said slowly and in great agony, "May God have mercy on your soul—and mine!" on which the muscles in my left arm stiffened. The big biceps—an heirloom of my athletic days—thickened up, and I turned my eyes away from the dying face, half hidden by the darkness. His struggles were very terrible, but with my weight upon his lower limbs, and my grasp upon his windpipe, that death-throe was as silent as it was horrible. The end came slowly. I could not bear the horror of it longer. I must finish it and be done with it. I put my right arm under the man's shoulders and raised the upper part of his body from the berth. Then a desperate wrench with my left arm, and there was a dull crack like the snapping of a dry stick. It was over. Rockingham's neck was broken.

I wiped away the bloody froth that oozed from the gaping mouth, and tried to compose decently the contorted figure. I covered the face. Then

I started on my last mission, for now I knew the door. I had bought the knowledge dearly, and I meant to use it for my own purpose, careless of what violence might be necessary to accomplish my end.

When I entered Brande's state-room I found the electric light full on. He was seated at a writing-table with his head resting on his arms, which hung crossways over the desk. The sleeper breathed so deeply it was evident that the effect of the morphia was still strong upon him. One hand clutched a folded parchment. His fingers clasped it nervelessly, and I had only to force them open one by one in order to withdraw the manu-script. As I did this, he moaned and moved in his chair. I had no fear of his awaking. My hand shook as I unfolded the parchment which I un-consciously handled as carefully as though the thing itself were as deadly as the destruction which might be wrought by its direction.

To me the whole document was a mass of unintelligible formulæ. My rusty university education could make nothing of it. But I could not waste time in trying to solve the puzzle, for I did not know what moment some other visitor might arrive to see how Brande fared.

I first examined with a pocket microscope the ink of the manuscript, and then making a scratch with Brande's pen on a page of my note-book, I compared the two. The colours were identical. It was the same ink.

In several places where a narrow space had been left vacant, I put 1 in front of the figures which followed. I had no reason for making this particular alteration, save that the figure 1 is more easily forged than any other, and the forgery is consequently more difficult to detect. My additions, when the ink was dry, could only have been discovered by one who was informed that the document had been tampered with. It was probable that a drawer which stood open with the keys in the lock was the place where Brande kept this paper ; where he would look for it on awaking. I locked it in the drawer and put the keys into his pocket.

There was something still to do with the sleeping man, whose brain compassed such marvellous powers. His telepathic faculty must be destroyed. I must keep him seriously ill, without killing him. As long as he remained alive his friends would never question his calculations, and the fiasco which was possible under any circumstances

would then be assured. I had with me an
Eastern drug, which I had bought from an
Indian fakir once in Murzapoor. The man was
an impostor, whose tricks did not impose on
me. But the drug, however he came by it, was
reliable. It was a poison which produced a
mild form of cerebritis that dulled but did not
deaden the mental powers. It acted almost
identically whether administered sub-cutaneously
or, of course in a larger dose, internally. I
brought it home with the intention of giving
it to a friend who was interested in vivisection.
I did not think that I myself should be the
first and last to experiment with it. It served
my purpose well.

The moment I pricked his skin, Brande moved
in his seat. My hand was on his throat. He
nestled his head down again upon his arms, and
drew a deep breath. Had he moved again that
breath would have been his last. I had been
so wrought upon by what I had already done
that night, I would have taken his life without
the slightest hesitation, if the sacrifice seemed
necessary.

When my operation was over, I left the room
and moved silently along the corridor till I came

to the ladder leading to the deck. Edith Metford was waiting for me as we had arranged. She was shivering in spite of the awful heat.

" Have you done it ? " she whispered.

" I have," I answered, without saying how much I had done. " Now you must retire— and rest easy. The formula won't work. I have put both it and Brande himself out of gear."

" Thank God ! " she gasped, and then a sudden faintness came over her. It passed quickly, and as soon as she was sufficiently restored, I begged her to go below. She pleaded that she could not sleep, and asked me to remain with her upon the deck. " It would be absurd to suppose that either of us could sleep this night," she very truly said. On which I was obliged to tell her plainly that she must go below. I had more to do.

" Can I help ? " she asked anxiously.

" No. If you could, I would ask you, for you are a brave girl. I have something now to get through which is not woman's work."

" Your work is my work," she answered. " What is it ? "

" I have to lower a body overboard without anyone observing me."

There was no time for discussion, so I told her at once, knowing that she would not give way otherwise. She started at my words, but said firmly :

"How will you do that unobserved by the 'watch'? Go down and bring up your—bring it up. I will keep the men employed." She went forward, and I turned again to the companion.

When I got back to Rockingham's cabin I took a sheet of paper and wrote, "Heat—Mad!" making no attempt to imitate his writing. I simply scrawled the words with a rough pen in the hope that they would pass as a message from a man who was hysterical when he wrote them. Then I turned to the berth and took up the body. It was not a pleasant thing to do. But it must be done.

I was a long time reaching the deck, for the arms and legs swung to and fro, and I had to move cautiously lest they should knock against the woodwork I had to pass. I got it safely up and hurried aft with it. Edith, I knew, would contrive to keep the men on watch engaged until I had disposed of my burden. I picked up a coil of rope and made it fast to the dead man's neck. Taking one turn of the rope round a boat-davit, I pushed the thing over the rail. I intended to let go the rope the moment the weight attached to it was safely in the sea, and so lowered away silently, paying out the line without excessive strain owing to the support of the davit round which I had wound it. I had not to wait so long as that, for just as the body was dangling over the foaming wake of the steamer, a little streak of moonlight shot out from behind a bank of cloud and lighted the vessel with a sudden gleam. I was startled by this, and held on, fearing that some watching eye might see my curious movements. For a minute I leaned over the rail and watched the track of the steamer as though I had come on deck for the air. There was a quick rush near the vessel's quarter. Something dark leaped out of the water, and there was a sharp snap—a crunch. The lower limbs were gone in the jaws of a shark. I let go the rope in horror, and the body dropped splashing into that hideous fishing-ground. Sick to death I turned away.

"Get below quickly," Edith Metford said in my ear. "They heard the splash, slight as it was, and are coming this way." Her warning was nearly a sob.

We hurried down the companion as fast as we dared, and listened to the comments of the watch above. They were soon satisfied that nothing of importance had occurred, and resumed their stations.

Before we parted on that horrible night, Edith said in a trembling voice, "You have done your work like a brave man."

"Say rather, like a forger and murderer," I answered.

"No," she maintained. "Many men before you have done much worse in a good cause. You are not a forger. You are a diplomat. You are not a murderer. You are a hero."

But I, being new to this work of slaughter and deception, could only deprecate her sympathy and draw away. I felt that my very presence near her was pollution. I was unclean, and I told her that I was so. Whereupon, without hesitation, she put her arms round my neck, and said clinging closely to me :

"You are not unclean—you are free from guilt. And—Arthur—I will kiss you now."

CHAPTER XV.

"IF NOT TOO LATE!"

WHEN I came on deck next morning the coast of Arabia was rising, a thin thread of hazy blue between the leaden grey of the sea and the soft grey of the sky. The morning was cloudy, and the blazing sunlight was veiled in atmospheric gauze. I had hardly put my foot on deck when Natalie Brande ran to meet me. I hung back guiltily.

"I thought you would never come. There is dreadful news!" she cried.

I muttered some incoherent words, to which she did not attend, but went on hurriedly:

"Rockingham has thrown himself overboard in a hysterical fit, brought on by the heat. The sailors heard the splash—"

"I know they did." This escaped me unawares, and I instantly prevaricated, "I have been told about that."

"Do you know that Herbert is ill?"

146

I could have conscientiously answered this question affirmatively also. Her sudden sympathy for human misadventure jarred upon me, as it had done once before, when I thought of the ostensible object of the cruise. I said harshly :

" Then Rockingham is at rest, and your brother is on the road to it." It was a brutal speech. It had a very different effect to that which I intended.

" True," she said. " But think of the awful consequences if, now that Rockingham is gone, Herbert should be seriously ill."

" I do think of it," I said stiffly. Indeed, I could hardly keep from adding that I had provided for it.

" You must come to him at once. I have faith in you." This gave me a twinge. " I have no faith in Percival " (the ship's doctor).

" You are nursing your brother ? " I said with assumed carelessness.

" Of course."

" What is Percival giving him ? "

She described the treatment, and as this was exactly what I myself would have prescribed to put my own previous interference right, I promised to come at once, saying :

"It is quite evident that Percival does not understand the case."

"That is exactly what I thought," Natalie agreed, leading me to Brande's cabin. I found his vitality lower than I expected, and he was very impatient. The whole purpose of his life was at stake, dependent on his preserving a healthy body, on which, in turn, a vigorous mind depends.

"How soon can you get me up?" he asked sharply, when my pretended examination was over.

"I should say a month at most."

"That would be too long," he cried. "You must do it in less."

"It does not depend on me—"

"It does depend on you. I know life itself. You know the paltry science of organic life. I have had no time for such trivial study. Get me well within three days, or—"

"I am attending."

"By the hold over my sister's imagination which I have gained, I will kill her on the fourth morning from now."

"You will—*not*."

"I tell you I will," Brande shrieked, starting up in his berth. "I could do it now."

" You could—*not.*"

" Man, do you know what you are saying ?
You to bandy words with me !   A clod-brained
fool to dare a man of science !   Man of science
forsooth !   Your men of science are to me as
brain-benumbed, as brain-bereft, as that fly which
I crush—thus ! "

The buzzing insect was indeed dead.   But I
was something more than a fly.   At last I was on
a fair field with this scientific magician or madman.   And on a fair field I was not afraid of
him.

" You are agitating yourself unnecessarily and
injuriously," I said in my best professional manner.   " And if you persist in doing so you will
make my one month three."

In a voice of undisguised scorn, Brande exclaimed, without noticing my interruption :

" Bearded by a creature whose little mind is to
me like the open page of a book to read when the
humour seizes me."   Then with a fierce glance at
me he cried :

" I have read your mind before.   I can read it
now."

" You can—*not.*"

He threw himself back in his berth and strove

to concentrate his mind. For nearly five minutes
he lay quite still, and then he said gently :

"You are right.   Have you, then, a higher
power than I ?"

"No ; a lower !"

"A lower ! What do you mean ?"

"I mean that I have merely paralysed your
brain—that for many months to come it will not
be restored to its normal power—that it will
never reach its normal power again unless I
choose."

"Then all is lost—lost—lost !" he wailed out.
"The end is as far off, and the journey as long,
and the way as hard, as if I had never striven.
And the tribute of human tears will be exacted
to the uttermost. My life has been in vain !"

The absolute agony in his voice, the note of
almost superhuman suffering and despair, was so
intense, that, without thinking of what it was
this man was grieving over, I found myself saying soothingly :

"No, no ! Nothing is lost. It is only your
own overstrained nervous system which sends
these fantastic nightmares to your brain. I will
soon make you all right if you will listen to
reason."

He turned to me with the most appealing look which I had ever seen in human eyes save once before—when Natalie pleaded with me.

"I had forgotten," he said, "the issue now lies in your hands. Choose rightly. Choose mercy."

"I will," I answered shortly, for his request brought me back with a jerk to his motive.

"Then you will get me well as soon as your skill can do it ?"

"I will keep you in your present condition until I have your most solemn assurance that you will neither go farther yourself nor instigate others to go farther with this preposterous scheme of yours."

"Bah !" Brande ejaculated contemptuously, and lay back with a sudden content. "My brain is certainly out of order, else I should not have forgotten—until your words recalled it—the Labrador expedition."

"The Labrador expedition ? "

"Yes. On the day we sailed for the Arafura Sea, Grey started with another party for Labrador. If we fail to act before the 31st December, in the year 2000, he will proceed. And the end of the century will be the date of the end of the earth. I will signal to him now."

His face changed suddenly. For a moment I thought he was dead. Then the dreadful fact came home to me. He was telegraphing telepathically to Grey. So the murder that was upon my soul had been done in vain. Then another life must be taken. Better a double crime than one resultless tragedy. I was spared this.

Brande opened his eyes wearily, and sighed as if fatigued. The effort, short as it was, must have been intense. He was prostrated. His voice was low, almost a whisper, as he said:

"You have succeeded beyond belief. I cannot even signal him, much less exchange ideas." With that he turned his face from me, and instantly fell into a deep sleep.

I left the cabin and went on deck. As usual, it was fairly sprinkled over with the passengers, but owing to the strong head-wind caused by the speed of the steamer, there was a little nook in the bow where there was no one to trouble me with unwelcome company.

I sat down on an arm of the starboard anchor and tried to think. The game which seemed so nearly won had all to be played over again from the first move. If I had killed Brande—which surely would have been justifiable—the other expedition would go on from where he left off. And how should I find them? And who would believe my story when I got back to England?

Brande must go on. His attempt to wreck the earth, even if the power he claimed were not overrated, would fail. For if the compounds of a common explosive must be so nicely balanced as they require to be, surely the addition of the figures which I had made in his formula would upset the balance of constituents in an agent so delicate, though so powerful, as that which he had invented. When the master failed, it was more than probable that the pupil would distrust the invention, and return to London for fresh experiments. Then a clean sweep must be made of the whole party. Meantime, it was plain that Brande must be allowed the opportunity of failing. And this it would be my hazardous duty to superintend.

I returned to Brande's cabin with my mind made up. He was awake, and looked at me eagerly, but waited for me to speak. Our conversation was brief, for I had little sympathy with my patient, and the only anxiety I experienced about his health was the hope that he would not die until he had served my purpose.

"I have decided to get you up," I said curtly.

"You have decided well," he answered, with equal coldness.

That was the whole interview—on which so much depended.

After this I did not speak to Brande on any subject but that of his symptoms, and before long he was able to come on deck. The month I spoke of as the duration of his illness was an intentional exaggeration on my part.

Rockingham was forgotten with a suddenness and completeness that was almost ghastly. The Society claimed to have improved the old maxim to speak nothing of the dead save what is good. Of the dead they spoke not at all. It is a callous creed, but in this instance it pleased me well.

We did not touch at Aden, and I was glad of it. The few attractions of the place, the diving boys and the like, may be a relief in ordinary sea voyages, but I was too much absorbed in my experiment on Brande to bear with patience any delay which served to postpone the crisis of my

scheme. I had treated him well, so far as his
bodily health went, but I deliberately continued
to tamper with his brain, so that any return of
his telepathic power was thus prevented. Indeed,
Brande himself was not anxious for such return.
The power was always exercised at an extreme
nervous strain, and it was now, he said, unnecessary to his purpose.

In consequence of this determination, I modified the already minute doses of the drug I was
giving him. This soon told with advantage on
his health. His physical improvement partly
restored his confidence in me, so that he followed
my instructions faithfully. He evidently recognised that he was in my power; that if I did
not choose to restore him fully no other man
could.

Of the ship's officers, Anderson, who was in
command, and Percival, the doctor, were men of
some individuality. The captain was a good
sailor and an excellent man of business. In the
first capacity, he was firm, exacting, and scrupulously conscientious. In the second, his conscience
was more elastic when he saw his way clear to
his own advantage. He had certain rigid rules
of conduct which he prided himself on observing

to the letter, without for a moment suspecting that their *raison d'etre* lay in his own interests. His commercial morality only required him to keep within the law. His final contract with myself was, I admit, faithfully carried out, but the terms of it would not have discredited the most predatory business man in London town.

Percival was the opposite pole of such a character. He was a clever man, who might have risen in his profession but for his easy-going indolence. I spent many an hour in his cabin. He was a sportsman and a skilled *raconteur.* His anecdotes helped to while the weary time away. He exaggerated persistently, but this did not disturb me. Besides, if in his narratives he lengthened out the hunt a dozen miles and increased the weight of the fish to an impossible figure, made the brace a dozen and the ten-ton boat a man-of-war, it was not because he was deliberately untruthful. He looked back on his feats through the telescope of a strongly magnifying memory. It was more agreeable to me to hear him boast his prowess than have him inquire after the health and treatment of my patient Brande. On this matter he was naturally very curious, and I very reticent.

That Brande did not entirely trust me was evident from his confusion when I surprised him
once reading his formula. His anxiety to con-
vince me that it was only a commonplace memorandum was almost ludicrous. I was glad to see
him anxious about that document. The more
carefully he preserved it, and the more faithfully
he adhered to its conditions, the better for my
experiment. A sense of security followed this
incident. It did not last long. It ended that
evening.

After a day of almost unendurable heat, I
went on deck for a breath of air. We were
well out in the Indian Ocean, and soundings
were being attempted by some of our naturalists. I sat alone and watched the sun sink
down into the glassy ocean on which our rushing
vessel was the only thing that moved. As the
darkness of that hot, still night gathered, weird
gleams of phosphorus broke from the steamer's
bows and streamed away behind us in long
lines of flashing spangles. Where the swell
caused by the passage of the ship rose in curling
waves, these, as they splashed into mimic
breakers, burst into showers of flamboyant light.
The water from the discharge-pipe poured down

in a cascade, that shone like silver. Every turn of the screw dashed a thousand flashes on either side, and the heaving of the lead was like the flight of a meteor, as it plunged with a luminous trail far down into the dark unfathomable depths below.

My name was spoken softly. Natalie Brande stood beside me. The spell was complete. The unearthly glamour of the magical scene had been compassed by her. She had called it forth and could disperse it by an effort of her will. I wrenched my mind free from the foolish phantasmagoria.

"I have good news," Natalie said in a low voice. Her tones were soft, musical; her manner caressing. Happiness was in her whole bearing, tenderness in her eyes. Dread oppressed me. "Herbert is now well again."

"He has been well for some time," I said, my heart beating fast.

"He is not thoroughly restored even yet. But this evening he was able to receive a message from me by the thought waves. He thinks you are plotting injury to him. His brain is not yet sufficiently strong to show how foolish this fugitive fancy is. Perhaps you would go to him.

He is troubling himself over this. You can set his mind at rest."

"I can—and will—if I am not too late," I answered.

CHAPTER XVI.

£5000 TO DETAIN THE SHIP.

BRANDE was asleep when I entered his cabin. His writing-table was covered with scraps of paper on which he had been scribbling. My name was on every scrap, preceded or followed by an unfinished sentence, thus: "Marcel is thinking— When I was ill, Marcel thought— Marcel means to—" All these I gathered up carefully and put in my pocket. Then I inoculated him with as strong a solution of the drug I was using on him as was compatible with the safety of his life. Immediate danger being thus averted, I determined to run no similar risk again.

For many days after this our voyage was monotonous. The deadly secret shared by Edith Metford and myself drew us gradually nearer to each other as time passed. She understood me, or, at least, gave me the impression that she understood me. Little by little that capricious mood which I have heretofore described changed into one of enduring sympathy. With one trivial exception, this lasted until the end. But for her help my mind would hardly have stood the strain of events which were now at hand, whose livid shadows were projected in the rising fire of Brande's relentless eyes.

Brande appeared to lose interest gradually in his ship's company. He became daily more and more absorbed in his own thoughts. Natalie was ever gentle, even tender. But I chafed at the impalpable barrier which was always between us. Sometimes I thought that she would willingly have ranged herself on my side. Some hidden power held her back. As to the others, I began to like the boy Halley. He was lovable, if not athletic. His devotion to Natalie, which never waned, did not now trouble me. It was only a friendship, and I welcomed it. Had it been anything more, it was not likely that he would have prevailed against the will of a man who had done murder for his mistress. We steamed through the Malay Archipelago, steering north, south, east, west, as if at haphazard, until only the navigating officers and the director of the Society knew how our course lay. We were searching for an island

L

about the bearings of which, it transpired, some mistake had been made. I do not know whether the great laureate ever sailed these seas. But I know that his glorious islands of flowers and islands of fruit, with all their luscious imagery, were here eclipsed by our own islands of foliage. The long lagoons, the deep blue bays, the glittering parti-coloured fish that swam in visible shoals deep down amidst the submerged coral groves over which we passed, the rich-toned sea-weeds and brilliant anemones, the yellow strands and the steep cliffs, the riotous foliage that swept down from the sky to the blue of the sea; all these natural beauties seemed to cry to me with living voices—to me bound on a cruise of universal death.

After a long spell of apparently aimless but glorious steaming, a small island was sighted on our port bow. The *Esmeralda* was steered directly for it, and we dropped anchor in a deep natural harbour on its southern shore. Preparations for landing had been going on during the day, and everything was ready for quitting the ship.

It was here that my first opportunity for making use of the gold I had brought with me occurred.

Anderson was called up by Brande, who made him a short complimentary speech, and finished it by ordering his officer to return to England, where further instructions would be given him. This order was received in respectful silence. Captain Anderson had been too liberally treated to demur if the *Esmeralda* had been ordered to the South Pole.

Brande went below for a few minutes, and as soon as he had disappeared I went forward to Anderson and hailed him nervously, for there was not a moment to spare.

" Anderson," I said hurriedly, " you must have noticed that Mr. Brande is an eccentric—"

" Pardon me, sir ; it is not my business to comment upon my owner."

" I did not ask you to comment upon him, sir," I said sharply. " It is I who shall comment upon him, and it is for you to say whether you will undertake to earn my money by waiting in this harbour till I am ready to sail back with you to England."

" Have you anything more to say, sir ? " Anderson asked stiffly.

" I presume I have said enough."

" If you have nothing more to say I must ask

you to leave the bridge, and if it were not that you are leaving the ship this moment, I would caution you not to be impertinent to me again."

He blew his whistle, and a steward ran forward.

"Johnson, see Mr. Marcel's luggage over the side at once." To me he said shortly: "Quit my ship, sir."

This trivial show of temper, which, indeed, had been provoked by my own hasty speech, turned my impatience into fury.

"Before I quit your ship," I said, with emphasis, "I will tell you how you yourself will quit it. You will do so between two policemen if you land in England, and between two marines if you think of keeping on the high seas. Before we started, I sent a detailed statement of this ship, the nature of this nefarious voyage, and the names of the passengers—or as many as I knew—to a friend who will put it in proper hands if anything befalls me. Go back without me and explain the loss of that French fishing fleet which was sunk the very night we sailed. It is an awkward coincidence to be explained by a man who returns from an unknown voyage having lost his entire list of passengers. You cannot be aware of what this man Brande intends, or you would at least stand by us as long as your own safety permitted. In any case you cannot safely return without us."

Anderson, after reflecting for a moment, apologised for his peremptory words, and agreed to stand by night and day, with fires banked, until I, and all whom I could prevail upon to return with me, got back to his vessel. There was no danger of his running short of coal. A ship that was practically an ocean liner in coal ballast would be a considerable time in burning out her own cargo. But he insisted on a large money payment in advance. I had foolishly mentioned that I had a little over £5000 in gold. This he claimed on the plea that "in duty to himself" —a favourite phrase of his—he could not accept less. But I think his sense of duty was limited only by the fact that I had hardly another penny in the world. Under the circumstances he might have waived all remuneration. As he was firm, and as I had no time to haggle, I agreed to give him the money. Our bargain was only completed when Brande returned to the deck.

It was strange that on an island like that

on which we were landing there should be a
regular army of natives waiting to assist us
with our baggage, and the saddled horses which
were in readiness were out of place in a primeval
wilderness. An Englishman came forward, and,
saluting Brande, said all was ready for the start
to the hills. This explained the puzzle. An
advance agent had made everything comfortable.
For Brande, his sister, and Miss Metford the
best appointed horses were selected. I, as
physician to the chief, had one. The main body
had to make the journey on foot, which they
did by very easy stages, owing to the heat and
the primitive track which formed the only road.
Their journey was not very long—perhaps ten
miles in a direct line.

Mounted as we were, it was often necessary
to stoop to escape the dense masses of parasitic
growth which hung in green festoons from every
branch of the trees on either side. Under this
thick shade all the riotous vegetation of the
tropics had fought for life and struggled for light
and air till the wealth of their luxuriant death
had carpeted the underwood with a thick de-
posit of steaming foliage. As we ascended the
height, every mile in distance brought changes

in the botanical growths, which might have passed unnoticed by the ordinary observer or ignorant pioneer. All were noted and commented on by Brande, whose eye was still as keen as his brain had once been brilliant. His usual staid demeanour changed suddenly. He romped ahead of us like a school-boy out for a holiday. Unlike a school-boy, however, he was always seeking new items of knowledge and conveying them to us with unaffected pleasure. He was more like a master who had found new ground and new material for his class. Natalie gave herself up like him to this enjoyment of the moment. Edith Metford and I partly caught the glamour of their infectious good-humour. But with both of us it was tempered by the knowledge of what was in store.

When we arrived at our destination we dismounted, at Brande's request, and tied our horses to convenient branches. He went forward, and, pushing aside the underwood with both hands, motioned to us to follow him till he stopped on a ledge of rock which overtopped a hollow in the mountain. The gorge below was the most beautiful glade I ever looked upon. ·

It was a paradise of foliage. Here and there a

fallen tree had formed a picturesque bridge over the mountain stream which meandered through it. Far down below there was a waterfall, where gorgeous tree-ferns rose in natural bowers, while others further still leant over the lotus-covered stream, their giant leaves trailing in the slow-moving current. Tangled masses of bracken rioted in wild abundance over a velvety green sod, overshadowed by waving magnolias. Through the trees bright-plumaged birds were flitting from branch to branch in songless flight, flashing their brilliant colours through the sunny leaves. In places the water splashed over moss-grown rocks into deep pools. Every drifting spray of cloud threw over the dell a new light, deepening the shadows under the great ferns.

It was here in this glorious fairyland; here upon this island, where before us no white foot had ever trod; whose nameless people represented the simplest types of human existence, that Herbert Brande was to put his devilish experiment to the proof. I marvelled that he should have selected so fair a spot for so terrible a purpose. But the papers which I found later amongst the man's effects on the *Esmeralda* explain much that was then incomprehensible to me.

Our camp was quickly formed, and our life was outwardly as happy as if we had been an ordinary company of tourists. I say outwardly, because, while we walked and climbed and collected specimens of botanical or geological interest, there remained that latent dread which always followed us, and dominated the most frivolous of our people, on all of whom a new solemnity had fallen. For myself, the fact that the hour of trial for my own experiment was daily drawing closer and more inevitable, was sufficient to account for my constant and extreme anxiety.

Brande joined none of our excursions. He was always at work in his improvised laboratory. The boxes of material which had been brought from the ship nearly filled it from floor to roof, and from the speed with which these were emptied, it was evident that their contents had been systematised before shipment. In place of the varied collection of substances there grew up within the room a cone of compound matter in which all were blended. This cone was smaller, Brande admitted, than what he had intended. The supply of subordinate fulminates, though several times greater than what was required, proved to be considerably short. But as he had allowed himself a large margin—everything being on a scale far exceeding the minimum which his calculations had pointed to as sufficient—this deficiency did not cause him more than a temporary annoyance. So he worked on.

When we had been three weeks on the island I found the suspense greater than I could bear. The crisis was at hand, and my heart failed me. I determined to make a last appeal to Natalie, to fly with me to the ship. Edith Metford would accompany us. The rest might take the risk to which they had consented.

I found Natalie standing on the high rock whence the most lovely view of the dell could be obtained, and as I approached her silently she was not aware of my presence until I laid my hand on her shoulder.

"Natalie," I said wistfully, for the girl's eyes were full of tears, "do you mind if I withdraw now from this enterprise, in which I cannot be of the slightest use, and of which I most heartily disapprove?"

"The Society would not allow you to withdraw. You cannot do so without its permission, and hope to live within a thousand miles of it," she answered gravely.

" I should not care to live within ten thousand miles of it. I should try to get and keep the earth's diameter between myself and it."

She looked up with an expression of such pain that my heart smote me. " How about me ? I cannot live without you now," she said softly.

"Don't live without me. Come with me. Get rid of this infamous association of lunatics, whose object they themselves cannot really appreciate, and whose means are murder—"

But there she stopped me. " My brother could find me out at the uttermost ends of the earth if I forsook him, and you know I do not mean to forsake him. For yourself—do not try to desert. It would make no difference. Do not believe that any consideration would cause me willingly to give you a moment's pain, or that I should shrink from sacrificing myself to save you." With one of her small white hands she gently pressed my head towards her. Her lips touched my forehead, and she whispered : " Do not leave me. It will soon be over now. I—I—need you."

As I was returning dejected after my fruitless

appeal to Natalie, I met Edith Metford, to whom I had unhappily mentioned my proposal for an escape.

"Is it arranged?   When do we start?" she asked eagerly.

"It is not arranged, and we do not start," I answered in despair.

"You told me you would go with her or without her," she cried passionately. "It is shameful —unmanly."

"It is certainly both if I really said what you tell me.   I was not myself at the moment, and my tongue must have slandered me.   I stay to the end.   But you will go.   Captain Anderson will receive you—"

"How am I to be certain of that?"

"I paid him for your passage, and have his receipt."

"And you really think I would go and leave —leave—"

"Natalie?   I think you would be perfectly justified."

At this the girl stamped her foot passionately on the ground and burst into tears.   Nor would she permit any of the slight caresses I offered.

I thought her old caprices were returning. She flung my arm rudely from her and left me bewildered.

CHAPTER XVII.

"THIS EARTH SHALL DIE."

MY memory does not serve me well in the scenes which immediately preceded the closing of the drama in which Brande was chief actor. It is doubtless the transcendental interest of the final situation which blunts my recollection of what occurred shortly before it. I did not abate one jot of my determination to fight my venture out unflinching, but my actions were probably more automatic than reasoned, as the time of our last encounter approached. On the whole, the fight had been a fair one. Brande had used his advantage over me for his own purpose as long as it remained with him. I used the advantage as soon as it passed to me for mine. The conditions had thus been equalised when, for the third and last time, I was to hear him address his Society.

174

This time the man was weak in health. His vitality was ebbing fast, but his marvellous inspiration was strong within him, and, supported by it, he battled manfully with the disease which I had manufactured for him. His lecture-room was the fairy glen; his canopy the heavens.

I cannot give the substance of this address, or any portion of it, verbatim as on former occasions, for I have not the manuscript. I doubt if Brande wrote out his last speech. Methodical as were his habits it is probable that his final words were not premeditated. They burst from him in a delirium that could hardly have been studied. His fine frenzy could not well have originated from considered sentences, although his language, regarded as mere oratory, was magnificent. It was appalling in the light through which I read it.

He stood alone upon the rock which overtopped the dell. We arranged ourselves in such groups as suited our inclinations, upon some rising ground below. The great trees waved overhead, low murmuring. The waterfall splashed drearily. Below, not a whisper was exchanged. Above, the man poured out his triumphant death-song in sonorous periods. Below, great fear was upon all. Above, the madman exulted wildly.

At first his voice was weak. As he went on it gained strength and depth. He alluded to his first address, in which he had hinted that the material Universe was not quite a success; to his second, in which he had boldly declared it was an absolute failure. This, his third declaration, was to tell us that the remedy as far as he, a mortal man, could apply it, was ready. The end was at hand. That night should see the consummation of his life-work. To-morrow's sun would rise—if it rose at all—on the earth restored to space.

A shiver passed perceptibly over the people, prepared as they were for this long foreseen announcement. Edith Metford, who stood by me on my left, slipped her hand into mine and pressed my fingers hard. Natalie Brande, on my right, did not move. Her eyes were dilated and fixed on the speaker. The old clairvoyante look was on her face. Her dark pupils were blinded save to their inward light. She was either unconscious or only partly conscious. Now that the hour had come, they who had believed their courage secure felt it wither. They, the people with us, begged for a little longer time to brace themselves for the great crisis—the plunge into an eternity from which there would be no resurrection, neither of matter nor of mind.

Brande heeded them not.

"This night," said he, with culminating enthusiasm, "the cloud-capped towers, the gorgeous palaces, the solemn temples, shall dissolve. To this great globe itself—this paltry speck of less account in space than a dew-drop in an ocean—and all its sorrow and pain, its trials and temptations, all the pathos and bathos of our tragic human farce, the end is near. The way has been hard, and the journey overlong, and the burden often beyond man's strength. But that long-drawn sorrow now shall cease. The tears will be wiped away. The burden will fall from weary shoulders. For the fulness of time has come. This earth shall die ! And death is peace.

"I stand," he cried out in a strident voice, raising his arm aloft, "I may say, with one foot on sea and one on land, for I hold the elemental secret of them both. And I swear by the living god—Science incarnate—that the suffering of the centuries is over, that for this earth and all that

M

it contains, from this night and for ever, *Time will be no more!*"

A great cry rose from the people. "Give us another day—only another day!"

But Brande made answer: "It is now too late."

"Too late!" the people wailed.

"Yes, too late. I warned you long ago. Are you not yet ready? In two hours the disintegrating agent will enter on its work. No human power could stop it now. Not if every particle of the material I have compounded were separated and scattered to the winds. Before I set my foot upon this rock I applied the key which will release its inherent energy. I myself am powerless."

"Powerless," sobbed the auditors.

"Powerless! And if I had ten thousand times the power which I have called forth from the universal element, I would use it towards the issue I have forecast."

Thereupon he turned away. Doom sounded in his words. The hand of Death laid clammy fingers on us. Edith Metford's strength failed at last. It had been sorely tested. She sank into my arms.

"Courage, true heart, our time has come," I whispered. "We start for the steamer at once. The horses are ready." My arrangements had been already made. My plan had been as carefully matured as any ever made by Brande himself.

"How many horses?"

"Three. One for you; another for Natalie; the third for myself. The rest must accept the fate they have selected."

The girl shuddered as she said, "But your interference with the formula? You are sure it will destroy the effect?"

"I am certain that the particular result on which Brande calculates will not take place. But short of that, he has still enough explosive matter stored to cause an earthquake. We are not safe within a radius of fifty miles. It will be a race against time."

"Natalie will not come."

"Not voluntarily. You must think of some plan. Your brain is quick. We have not a moment to lose. Ah, there she is! Speak to her."

Natalie was crossing the open ground which led from the glen to Brande's laboratory. She did not observe us till Edith called to her. Then she approached hastily and embraced her friend with visible emotion. Even to me she offered her cheek without reserve.

"Natalie," I said quickly, "there are three horses saddled and waiting in the palm grove. The *Esmeralda* is still lying in the harbour where we landed. You will come with us. Indeed, you have no choice. You must come if I have to carry you to your horse and tie you to the saddle. You will not force me to put that indignity upon you. To the horses, then! Come!"

For answer she called her brother loudly by his name. Brande immediately appeared at the door of his laboratory, and when he perceived from whom the call had come he joined us.

"Herbert," said Natalie, "our friend is deserting us. He must still cling to the thought that your purpose may fail, and he expects to escape on horseback from the fate of the earth. Reason with him yet a little further."

"There is no time to reason," I interrupted. "The horses are ready. This girl (pointing as I spoke to Edith Metford) takes one, I another, and you the third—whether your brother agrees or not."

'Surely you have not lost your reason? Have you forgotten the drop of water in the English Channel?'" Brande said quietly.

"Brande," I answered, "the sooner you induce your sister to come with me the better; and the sooner you induce these maniac friends of yours to clear out the better, for your enterprise will fail."

"It is as certain as the law of gravitation. With my own hand I mixed the ingredients according to the formula."

"And," said I, "with my own hand I altered your formula."

Had Brande's heart stopped beating, his face could not have become more distorted and livid. He moved close to me, and, glaring into my eyes, hissed out:

"You altered my formula?"

"I did," I answered recklessly. "I multiplied your figures by ten where they struck me as insufficient."

"When?"

I strode closer still to him and looked him straight in the eyes while I spoke.

"That night in the Red Sea, when Edith Metford, by accident, mixed morphia in your medicine,

The night I injected a subtle poison, which I picked up in India once, into your blood while you slept, thereby baffling some of the functions of your extraordinary brain. The night when in your sleep you stirred once, and had you stirred twice, I would have killed you, then and there, as ruthlessly as you would kill mankind now. The night I did kill your lieutenant, Rockingham, and throw his body overboard to the sharks."

Brande did not speak for a moment. Then he said in a gentle, uncomplaining voice :

" So it now devolves on Grey. The end will be the same. The Labrador expedition will succeed where I have failed." To Natalie : " You had better go. There will only be an explosion. The island will probably disappear. That will be all."

" Do you remain ? " she asked.

" Yes. I perish with my failure."

" Then I perish with you. And you, Marcel, save yourself—you coward ! "

I started as if struck in the face. Then I said to Edith : " Be careful to keep to the track. Take the bay horse. I saddled him for myself, but you can ride him safely. Lose no time, and ride hard for the coast."

"Arthur Marcel," she answered, so softly that the others did not hear, "your work in the world is not yet over. There is the Labrador expedition. Just now, when my strength failed, you whispered 'courage.' Be true to yourself! Half an hour is gone."

At length some glimmer of human feeling awoke in Brande. He said in a low, abstracted voice : "My life fittingly ends now. To keep you, Natalie, would only be a vulgar murder." The old will power seemed to come back to him. He looked into the girl's eyes, and said slowly and sternly : "Go! I command it."

Without another word he turned away from us. When he had disappeared into the laboratory, Natalie sighed, and said dreamily :

"I am ready. Let us go."

CHAPTER XVIII.

THE FLIGHT

I LED the girls hurriedly to the horses. When they were mounted on the ponies, I gave the bridle-reins of the bay horse—whose size and strength were necessary for my extra weight—to Edith Metford, and asked her to wait for me until I announced Brande's probable failure to the people, and advised a *sauve qui peut*.

Hard upon my warning there followed a strange metamorphosis in the crowd, who, after the passing weakness at the lecture, had fallen back into stoical indifference, or it may have been despair. The possibility of escape galvanized them into the desire for life. Cries of distress, and prayers for help, filled the air. Men and women rushed about like frightened sheep without concert or any sensible effort to escape, wasting in futile scrambles the short time remaining to them. For another half hour had now passed, and in sixty minutes the earthquake would take place.

" Follow us!" I shouted, as with my companions I rode slowly through the camp. " Keep the track to the sea. I shall have the steamer's boats ready for all who may reach the shore alive."

" The horses! Seize the horses!" rose in a loud shout, and the mob flung themselves upon us, as though three animals could carry all.

When I saw the rush, I called out: " Sit firm, Natalie; I am going to strike your horse." Saying which I struck the pony a sharp blow with my riding-whip crossways on the flank. It bounded like a deer, and then dashed forward down the rough pathway.

" Now you, Edith!" I struck her pony in the same way; but it only reared and nearly threw her. It could not get away. Already hands were upon both bridle-reins. There was no help for it. I pulled out my revolver and fired once, twice, and thrice—for I missed the second shot—and then the maddened animal sprang forward, released from the hands that held it.

It was now time to look to myself. I was in the midst of a dozen maniacs mad with fear.

I kicked in my spurs desperately, and the bay lashed out his hind feet. One hoof struck young Halley on the forehead. He fell back dead, his skull in fragments. But the others refused to break the circle. Then I emptied my weapon on them, and my horse plunged through the opening, followed by despairing execrations. The moment I was clear, I returned my revolver to its case, and settled myself in the saddle, for, borne out of the proper path as I had been, there was a stiff bank to leap before I could regain the track to the shore. Owing to the darkness the horse refused to leap, and I nearly fell over his head. With a little scrambling I managed to get back into my seat, and then trotted along the bank for a hundred yards. At this point the bank disappeared, and there was nothing between me now and the open track to the sea.

Once upon the path, I put the bay to a gallop, and very soon overtook a man and a woman hurrying on. They were running hand in hand, the man a little in front dragging his companion on by force. It was plain to me that the woman could not hold out much longer. The man, Claude Lureau, hailed me as I passed.

"Help us, Marcel. Don't ride away from us."

"I cannot save both," I answered, pulling up.

"Then save Mademoiselle Véret. I'll take my chance."

This blunt speech moved me, the more especially as the man was French. I could not allow him to point the way of duty to me—an Englishman.

"Assist her up, then. Now, Mademoiselle, put your arms round me and hold hard for your life. Lureau, you may hold my stirrup if you agree to loose it when you tire."

"I will do so," he promised.

Hampered thus, I but slowly gained on Natalie and Edith, whose ponies had galloped a mile before they could be stopped.

"Forward, forward!" I shouted when within hail. "Don't wait for me. Ride on at top speed. Lash your ponies with the bridle-reins."

We were all moving on now at an easy canter, for I could not go fast so long as Lureau held my stirrup, and the girls in front did not seem anxious to leave me far behind. Besides, the tangled underwood and overhanging creepers rendered hard riding both difficult and dangerous. The ponies were hard held, but notwithstanding this my horse fell back gradually in the race, and the hammering of the hoofs in front grew fainter. The breath of the runner at my stirrup came in great sobs. He was suffocating, but he struggled on a little longer. Then he threw up his hand and gasped :

"I am done. Go on, Marcel. You deserve to escape. Don't desert the girl."

"May God desert me if I do," I answered. "And do you keep on as long as you can. You may reach the shore after all."

"Go on—save her!" he gasped, and then from sheer exhaustion fell forward on his face.

"Sit still, Mademoiselle," I cried, pulling the French girl's arms round me in time to prevent her from throwing herself purposely from the horse. Then I drove in my spurs hard, and, being now released from Lureau's grasp, I overtook the ponies.

For five minutes we all rode on abreast. And then the darkness began to break, and a strange dawn glimmered over the tree-tops, although the hour of midnight was still to come. A wild, red light, like that of a fiery sunset in a hazy summer evening, spread over the night sky. The

quivering stars grew pale. Constellation after
constellation, they were blotted out until the
whole arc of heaven was a dull red glare. The
horses were dismayed by this strange phenomenon,
and dashed the froth from their foaming muzzles
as they galloped now without stress of spur at
their best speed. Birds that could not sing
found voice, and chattered and shrieked as they
dashed from tree to tree in aimless flight.
Enormous bats hurtled in the air, blinded by
the unusual light. From the dense undergrowth
strange denizens of the woods, disturbed in their
nightly prowl, leaped forth and scurried squeal-
ing between the galloping hoofs, reckless of
anything save their own fear. Everything that
was alive upon the island was in motion, and
fear was the motor of them all.

So far, we saw no natives. Their absence did
not surprise me, for I had no time for thought.
It was explained later.

Edith Metford's pony soon became unmanage-
able in its fright. I unbuckled one spur and
gave it to her, directing her to hold it in her
hand, for of course she could not strap it to her
boot, and drive it into the animal when he

swerved. She took the spur, and as her pony, in one of his side leaps, nearly bounded off the path, she struck him hard on the ribs. He bolted and flew on far ahead of us.

The light grew stronger.

But that the rays were red, it would now have been as bright as day. We were chasing our shadows, so the light must be directly behind us. Mademoiselle Véret first noticed this, and drew my attention to it. I looked back, and my heart sank at the sight. In the terror it inspired, I regretted having burthened myself with the girl I had sworn to save.

The island was on fire!

"It is the end of the world," Mademoiselle Véret said with a shudder. She clung closer to me. I could feel her warm breath upon my cheek. The unmanly regret, which for a moment had touched me, passed.

The ponies now seemed to find out that their safety lay in galloping straight on, rather than in scared leaps from side to side. They stretched themselves like race horses, and gave my bay, with his double burthen, a strong lead. The pace became terrible considering the nature of the ground we covered.

At last the harbour came in view. But my horse, I knew, could not last another mile, and the shore was still distant two or three. I spurred him hard and drew nearly level with the ponies, so that my voice could be heard by both their riders.

"Ride on," I shouted, "and hail the steamer, so that there may be no delay when I come up. This horse is blown, and will not stand the pace. I am going to ease him. You will go on board at once, and send the boat back for us." Then I eased the bay, but in spite of this I immediately overtook Edith Metford, who had pulled up.

My reproaches she cut short by saying, "If that horse does the distance at all it will be by getting a lead all the way. And I am going to give it to him." So we started together.

Natalie was waiting for us a little further on. I spoke to her, but she did not answer. From the moment that Brande had commanded her to accompany us, her manner had remained absolutely passive. What I ordered, she obeyed. That was all. Instead of being alarmed by the horrors of the ride, she did not seem to be even interested. I had not leisure, however, to reflect on this. For the first time in the whole race she spoke to us.

"Would it not be better if Edith rode on?" she said. "I can take her place. It seems useless to sacrifice her. It does not matter to me. I cannot now be afraid."

"I am afraid; but I remain," Edith said resolutely.

The ground under us began to heave. Whole acres of it swayed disjointed. We were galloping on oscillating fragments, which trembled beneath us like floating logs under boys at play. To jump these cracks—sometimes an upward bank, sometimes a deep drop, in addition to the width of the seam, had to be taken—pumped out the failing horses, and the hope that was left to us disappeared utterly.

The glare of the red light behind waxed fiercer still, and a low rumbling as of distant thunder began to mutter round us. The air became difficult to breathe. It was no longer air, but a mephitic stench that choked us with disgusting fumes. Then a great shock shook the land, and right in front of us a seam opened that must have been fully fifteen feet in width. Natalie was the first to see it. She observed it too late to stop.

In the same mechanical way as she had acted before, she settled herself in the saddle, struck the pony with her hand, and raced him at the chasm. He cleared it with little to spare. Edith's took it next with less. Then my turn came. Before I could shake up my tired horse, Mademoiselle Véret said quickly:

"Monsieur has done enough. He will now permit me to alight. This time the horse cannot jump over with both."

"He shall jump over with both, Mademoiselle, or he shall jump in," I answered. "Don't look down when we are crossing."

The horse just got over, but he came to his knees, and we fell forward over his shoulder. The girl's head struck full on a slab of rock, and a faint moan was all that told me she was alive as I arose half stunned to my feet. My first thought was for the horse, for on him all depended. He was uninjured, apparently, but hardly able to stand from the shock and the stress of fatigue.

Edith Metford had dismounted and caught him; she was holding the bridle in her left hand, and winced as if in pain when I accidentally brushed against her right shoulder. I tied the horse to a

N

young palm, and begged the girl to ride on. She obeyed me reluctantly. Natalie had to assist her to remount, so she must have been injured. When I saw her safely in her saddle, I ran back to Mademoiselle Véret.

The chasm was fast widening. From either side great fragments were breaking off and falling in with a roar of loose rocks crashing together, till far down the sound was dulled into a hollow boom. This ended in low guttural, which growled up from an abysmal depth. Mademoiselle Véret, or her dead body, lay now on the very edge of the seam, and I had to harden my heart before I could bring myself to venture close to it. But I had given my word, and there were no conditions in the promise when I made it.

I was spared the ordeal. Just as I stepped forward, the slab of rock on which the girl lay broke off in front of me, and, tipping up, over-turned itself into the chasm. Far below I could see the shimmer of the girl's dress as her body went plunging down into that awful pit. And remembering her generous courage and offer of self-sacrifice, I felt tears rise in my eyes. But there was no time for tears.

I leaped on the bay, and got him into something approaching a gallop, shouting at the others to keep on, for they were now returning. When I came up with them, Edith Metford said with a shiver :

" The girl ? "

" Is at the bottom of the pit. Ride on."

We gained the shore at last ; and our presence there produced the explanation of the absence of the natives on the pathway to the sea. They were there before us. Lying prostrate on the beach in hundreds, they raised their bodies partly from the sands, like a resurrection of the already dead, and there then rang out upon the night air a sound such as my ears had never before heard in my life, such as, I pray God, they may never listen to again. I do not know what that dreadful death-wail meant in words, only that it touched the lowest depths of human horror. All along the beach that fearful chorus of the damned wailed forth, and echoed back from rock and cliff. The cry for mercy could not be mistaken—the supplication blended with despair. They were praying to us—their evil spirits, for this wrong had been wrought them by our advent, if not by ourselves.

I cannot dwell upon the scene. I could not describe it. I would not if I could.

The steamer was still in her berth; her head was pointed seawards. Loud orders rang over the water. The roar of the chain running out through the hawse-hole and the heavy splash could not be mistaken. Anderson had slipped his cable. Then the chime of the telegraph on the bridge was followed almost instantly by the first smashing stroke of the propeller.

The *Esmeralda* was under weigh!

CHAPTER XIX.

THE CATASTROPHE.

THE *Esmeralda* was putting out to sea when I thought of a last expedient to draw the attention of her captain. Filling my revolver with cartridges which I had loose in my pockets, I fired all the chambers as fast as I could snap the trigger.

My signals were heard, and Anderson proved true to his bargain. He immediately reversed his engines, and, when he had backed in as close as he thought safe, sent a boat ashore for us. We got into it without any obstruction from the cowering natives, who only shrank from us in horror, now that their prayers had failed to move us. The moment our boat was made fast to the steamer's davit ropes and we were pulled out of the water, "full speed ahead" was rung from the bridge. We were raised to the deck while the vessel was getting up speed.

I crawled up the ladder to the bridge feebly, for I was becoming stiff from the bruises of the fall from my horse. Anderson received me coldly, and listened indifferently to my thanks. An agreement such as ours hardly prepared me for his loyalty.

"Oh, as to that," he interrupted, "when I make a bargain my word is my bond. On this occasion I am inclined to think the indenture will be a final one."

His bargain was a hard one, but, having made it, he abided faithfully by its conditions. He was honest, therefore, in his own way.

"How far can you get out in fifteen minutes?" I asked.

"We may make six or seven knots. But what is the good of that? There will be an earthquake on that island on a liberal scale—on such a scale that this ship would have very little chance in the wave that will follow us if we were fifty miles at sea."

"You have taken every precaution, of course—"

Anderson here looked at me contemptuously, and, with an air of sarcastic admiration, he said :

"You have guessed it at the first try. That is precisely what I have done."

"Pshaw! don't take offence at trifles at a time like this," I said testily. "If you knew as much about that earthquake as I do, you would be in no humour for bandying phrases."

"Might I ask how much you do know about it? You could not have foreseen the trouble more clearly if you had made it yourself."

"I did not make it myself, but I know the means which the man who did employed, and but for me that earthquake would have wrecked this earth."

Anderson made no direct answer to this, but he said earnestly:

"You will now go below, sir. You are done up. Roberts will take you to the doctor."

"I am not done up, and I mean to see it out," I retorted doggedly. My nervous system was completely unhinged, and a fit of stupid obstinacy came on me which rendered any interference with my actions intolerable.

"Then you cannot see it out upon my bridge," Anderson said. The determined tone in which he spoke only added to my impotent wrath.

"Very well, I will return to the deck, and if

any of your men should attempt to interfere with
me he will do so at his peril." With that, I
slung my revolver round so as to have it ready
to my hand. I was beside myself. My conduct
was already bad enough, but I made it worse
before I left the bridge.

"And if you, Anderson, disobey my orders
—my orders, do you hear?—an explosion such
as took place in the middle of the English
channel shall take place in the middle of this
ship."

"For God's sake leave the bridge. I want my
wits about me, and I have no intention of earn-
ing another exhibition of your devilries."

"Then be careful not to trouble me again."
Thus after having passed through much danger
with a spirit not unbecoming—as I hope—an
English gentleman, I acted, when the worst was
passed, like a peevish schoolboy. I am ashamed
of my conduct in this small matter, and trust it
will pass without much notice in the narrative
of events of greater moment.

On deck, Natalie Brande, Edith Metford, and
Percival were standing together, their eyes fixed
on the island. Edith's face was deathly white,
even in the ruddy glow which was now over

land and sea. When I saw her pallor, my evil temper passed away.

"It would be impossible for you to be quite well," I said to her anxiously ; "but has anything happened since I left you ?   You are very pale."

"Oh no," she answered, "I'm all right; a little faint after that ride.   I shall be better soon."

Natalie turned her weird eyes on me and said in the hollow voice we had heard once before—when she spoke to us on the island—"That is her way of telling you that your horse broke her right arm when she caught him for you. She held him, you remember, with her left hand. The doctor has set the limb.   She will not suffer long."

"Heaven help us, this awful night," Edith cried. "How do you know that, Natalie ? "

"I know much now, but I shall know more soon." After this she would not speak again.

With every pound of steam on that the *Esmeralda's* boilers would bear without bursting, we were now plunging through the great rollers of the Arafura Sea.   Everything had indeed been done to put the vessel in trim.   She was cleared for action, so to speak.   And a gallant fight she made when the issue was knit.   When the hour of midnight must be near at hand, I looked at my watch. It was one minute to twelve o'clock.

Thirty seconds more!

The stupendous corona of flame which hung over the island was pierced by long lines of smoke that stretched far above the glare and clutched with sooty fingers at the stars, now fitfully coming back to view at our distance. The rumbling of internal thunder waxed louder.

Fifteen seconds now!

Fearful peals rent the atmosphere. Vast tongues of flame protruded heavenward. The elements must be melting in that fervent heat. The blazing bowels of the earth were pouring forth.

Twelve, midnight!

A reverberation thundered out which shook the solid earth, and a roaring hell-breath of flame and smoke belched up so awful in its dread magnificence that every man who saw it and lived to tell his story might justly have claimed to have seen perdition. In that hurricane of incandescent matter the island was blotted out for ever from the map of this world.

Notwithstanding the speed of the *Esmeralda* she was a sloth when compared with the speed of the wave from such an earthquake. From the glare of the illumination to perfect darkness the contrast was sudden and extreme. But the blackness of the ocean was soon whitened by the snowy plumes of the avalanche of water which was now racing us, far astern as yet, but gaining fast. I, who had no business about the ship requiring my presence in any special part, decided to wait on deck and lash myself to the forward, which would be practically the lee-side of a deck-house. Edith Metford we prevailed on to go below, that she might not run the risk of further injury to her fractured arm. As she left us she whispered to me, "So Natalie will be with you at the end, and I—" a sob stopped her. And it came into my mind at that moment that this girl had acted very nobly, and that I had hardly appreciated her and all that she had done for me.

Natalie refused to leave the deck. I lashed her securely beside me. Together we awaited the end. When the roar of the following wave came close, so close that the voices of the officers of the ship could be no longer heard, Natalie spoke. The hollow sound was no longer in her voice. Her own soft sweet tones had come back.

" Arthur," she asked, " is this the end ? "

"I fear it is," I answered, speaking close to her ear so that she might hear.

"Then we have little time, and I have something which I must say, which you must promise me to remember when—when—I am no longer with you."

" You will be always with me while we live. I think I deserve that at last."

" Yes, you deserve that and more. I will be with you while I live, but that will not be for long."

I was about to interrupt her when she put her soft little hand upon my lips and said :

"Listen, there is very little time. It is all a mistake. I mean Herbert was wrong. He might as well have let me have my earthly span of happiness or folly—call it what you will."

" You see that now—thank God ! "

" Yes, but I see it too late, I did not know it until —until I was dead. Hush ! " Again I tried to interrupt her, for I thought her mind was wandering. "I died psychically with Herbert. That was when we first saw the light on the island. Since then I have lived mechanically, but it has only been life in so low a form that I do not now know what has happened between that time and this.

And I could not now speak as I am speaking save by a will power which is costing me very dear. But it is the only voice you could hear. I do not therefore count the cost. My brother's brain so far overmatched my own that it first absorbed and finally destroyed my mental vitality. This influence removed, I am a rudderless ship at sea—bound to perish."

" May his torments endure for ever. May the nethermost pit of hell receive him ! " I said with a groan of agony.

But Natalie said : " Hush ! I might have lingered on a little longer, but I chose to concentrate the vital force which would have lasted me a few more senile years into the minutes necessary for this message from me to you—a message I could not have given you if he were not dead. And I am dying so that you may hear it. Dying ! My God ! I am already dead."

She seemed to struggle against some force that battled with her, and the roar of many waters was louder around us before she was able to speak again.

" Bend lower, Arthur ; my strength is failing, and I have not yet said that for which I am here. Lower still.

" I said it is all a mistake—a hideous mistake. Existence as we know it is ephemeral. Suffering is ephemeral. There is nothing everlasting but love. There is nothing eternal but mind. Your mind is mine. Your love is mine. Your human life may belong to whomsoever you will it. It ought to belong to that brave girl below. I do not grudge it to her, for I have *you*. We two shall be together through the ages—for ever and for ever. Heart of my heart, you have striven manfully and well, and if you did not altogether succeed in saving my flesh from premature corruption, be satisfied in that you have my soul. Ah ! "

She pressed her hands to her head as if in dreadful pain. When she spoke again her voice came in short gasps.

" My brain is reeling. I do not know what I am saying," she cried, distraught. " I do not know whether I am saying what is true or only what I imagine to be true. I know nothing but this. I was mesmerised. I have been so for two years. But for that I would have been happy in your love—for I was a woman before this hideous influence benumbed me. They told me it was only a fool's paradise that I missed. But I only know that I have missed it. Missed it—and the darkness of death is upon me."

She ceased to speak. A shudder convulsed her, and then her head sank gently on my shoulder.

At that moment the great wave broke over the vessel, whirling her helpless like a cork on the ripples of a mill pond; lashing her with mighty strokes; sweeping in giant cataracts from stern to stem; smashing, tearing everything; deluging her with hissing torrents; crushing her with avalanches of raging foam. Then the ocean tornado passed on and left the *Esmeralda* behind, with half the crew disabled and many lost, her decks a mass of wreckage, her masts gone. The crippled ship barely floated. When the last torrent of spray passed, and I was able to look to Natalie, her head had drooped down on her breast. I raised her face gently and looked into her wide open eyes.

She was dead.

CHAPTER XX.

CONCLUSION.

TAKING up my girl's body in my arms, I stumbled over the wreck-encumbered deck, and bore it to the state-room she had occupied on the outward voyage. Percival was too busy attending to wounded sailors to be interrupted. His services, I knew, were useless now, but I wanted him to refute or corroborate a conviction which my own medical knowledge had forced upon me. The thought was so repellent, I clung to any hope which might lead to its dispersion. I waited alone with my dead.

Percival came after an hour, which seemed to me an eternity. He stammered out some incoherent words of sympathy as soon as he looked in my face. But this was not the purpose for which I had detached him from his pressing duties elsewhere. I made a gesture towards the dead girl.

He attended to it immediately. I watched closely and took care that the light should be on his face, so that I might read his eyes rather than listen to his words.

"She has fainted!" he exclaimed, as he approached the rigid figure. I said nothing until he turned and faced me. Then I read his eyes. He said slowly: "You are aware, Marcel, that—that she is dead ?"

"I am."

"That she has been dead—several hours ?"

"I am."

"But let me think. It was only an hour—"

"No; do not think," I interrupted. "There are things in this voyage which will not bear to be thought of. I thank you for coming so soon. You will forgive me for troubling you when you have so much to do elsewhere. And now leave us alone. I mean, leave me alone."

He pressed my hand, and went away without a word. I am that man's friend.

They buried her at sea.

I was happily unconscious at the time, and so was spared that scene. Edith Metford, weak and suffering as she was, went through it all. She has told me nothing about it, save that it was done. More than that I could not bear. And I have borne much.

The voyage home was a dreary episode. There is little more to tell, and it must be told quickly. Percival was kind, but it distressed me to find that he now plainly regarded me as weak-minded from the stress of my trouble. Once, in the extremity of my misery, I began a relation of my adventures to him, for I wanted his help. The look upon his face was enough for me. I did not make the same mistake again.

To Anderson I made amends for my extravagant display of temper. He received me more kindly than I expected. I no longer thought of the money that had passed between us. And, to do him tardy justice, I do not think he thought of it either. At least he did not offer any of it back. His scruples, I presume, were conscientious. Indeed, I was no longer worth a man's enmity. Sympathy was now the only indignity that could be put upon me. And Anderson did not trespass in that direction. My misery was, I thought, complete. One note must still be struck in that long discord of despair.

We were steaming along the southern coast of Java. For many hours the rugged cliffs and giant rocks which fence the island against the onslaught of the Indian Ocean had passed before us as in review, and we—Edith Metford and I—sat on the deck silently, with many thoughts in common, but without the interchange of a spoken word. The stern, forbidding aspect of that iron coast increased the gloom which had settled on my brain. Its ramparts of lonely sea-drenched crags depressed me below the mental zero that was now habitual with me. The sun went down in a red glare, which moved me not. The short twilight passed quickly, but I noticed nothing. Then night came. The restless sea disappeared in darkness. The grand march past of the silent stars began. But I neither knew nor cared.

A soft whisper stirred me.

"Arthur, for God's sake rouse yourself! You are brooding a great deal too much. It will destroy you."

Listlessly I put my hand in hers, and clasped her fingers gently.

"Bear with me!" I pleaded.

"I will bear with you for ever. But you must fight on. You have not won yet."

"No, nor ever shall. I have fought my last fight. The victory may go to whosoever desires it."

On this she wept. I could not bear that she should suffer from my misery, and so, guarding carefully her injured arm, I drew her close to me. And then, out of the darkness of the night, far over the solitude of the sea, there came to us the sound of a voice. That voice was a woman's wail. The girl beside me shuddered and drew back. I did not ask her if she had heard. I knew she had heard.

We arose and stood apart without any explanation. From that moment a caress would have been a sacrilege. I did not hear that weird sound again, nor aught else for an hour or more save the bursting of the breakers on the crags of Java.

I kept no record of the commonplaces of our

voyage thereafter. It only remains for me to say that I arrived in England broken in health and bankrupt in fortune. Brande left no money. His formula for the transmutation of metals is unintelligible to me. I can make no use of it.

Edith Metford remains my friend. To part utterly after what we have undergone together is beyond our strength. But between us there is a nameless shadow, reminiscent of that awful night in the Arafura Sea, when death came very near to us. And in my ears there is always the echo of that voice which I heard by the shores of Java when the misty borderland between life and death seemed clear.

My story is told. I cannot prove its truth, for there is much in it to which I am the only living witness. I cannot prove whether Herbert Brande was a scientific magician possessed of *all* the powers he claimed, or merely a mad physicist in charge of a new and terrible explosive; nor whether Edward Grey ever started for Labrador. The burthen of the proof of this last must be borne by others — unless it be left to Grey himself to show whether my evidence is false or true. If it be left to him, a few years will decide the issue.

I am content to wait.

THE END.

LONDON : DIGBY, LONG AND CO., PUBLISHERS, 18 BOUVERIE STREET, FLEET STREET, E.C.

ROBERT CROMIE'S BOOKS

OPINIONS OF THE PRESS

A PLUNGE INTO SPACE

WITH PREFACE BY JULES VERNE

Times.—The story is written with considerable liveliness, the scientific jargon is sufficiently perplexing, and the characters are sketched with some humour.

Chronicle.—A strange, weird, mysterious story that holds the reader spell-bound, from the first page to the last.

Athenæum.—Mr. Cromie's Utopia is charming, and the quasi-scientific detail of the expedition is given with so much integrity that we hardly wonder at the marvellous results accomplished.

Truth.—A very clever description of a flight through space to Mars . . . . the book is extremely interesting and suggestive ; especially, perhaps, where it attacks the theories of Mr. George and " Looking Backwards."

Court Journal.—Mr. Robert Cromie's remarkably clever and enter-taining volume is told with much of the vivid fancy of a Jules Verne—with remarkable picturesqueness, and the experiences of mortals in Mars are described with considerable humour.

Review of Reviews.—An unquestionably interesting story. The adventures of the hero and his friends are in no small degree thrilling.

Glasgow Herald.—The imagination is brilliant, the scientific details are skilfully worked in, the dialogues and descriptions are lively and interesting, and the pictures of Martian life and scenery are remarkable —a decidedly clever book.

FOR ENGLAND'S SAKE

Academy.—There is not a dull page in the story.

Army and Navy Gazette.—A capital little story of military life, full of bright word-painting.

Literary World.—This exciting chapter in the history of the future is written with a great deal of enthusiasm, and a great deal of common sense to boot.

Irish Times.—The plot is well conceived, and the interest throughout is well maintained.

Belfast Northern Whig.—The author displays much constructive and descriptive power. He is most felicitous in his word pictures of scenery, and imparts a fascinating dash to his military scenes.

Belfast Morning News.—Deeply interesting without being sensational, this charming story of love and war is sure to appeal with force to a large circle of readers.

Liverpool Daily Post.—A well-told story of life and love in troublous times in India.

IN SOUTHERN SEAS

WRITTEN IN COLLABORATION WITH W. R. RINGLAND.

Athenæum.—A bright, compact, and highly readable narrative, full of incidents, and illustrated with clever little vignettes.

Newcastle Chronicle.—A really charming book—deeply interesting, and full of capital drawings.

Scotsman.—A very well-written narrative of a trip, and as such, about as good as it could be.

Spectator.—A pleasant little book of travel.

Leeds Mercury.—The author relies on vivid description, pointed and racy pictures, and lively and striking incident for interest.

Saturday Review.—Brightly written, and yet more brightly illustrated.

The foregoing Books may be had through DIGBY, LONG & CO., 18 BOUVERIE STREET, FLEET STREET, LONDON, E.C.

SUPPLEMENTARY LIST

DIGBY, LONG & CO.'S
NEW NOVELS, STORIES, Etc.

IN ONE VOLUME, Price 6s.

NEW NOVEL BY DR ARABELLA KENEALY.

The Honourable Mrs Spoor. By the Author of "Some Men are such Gentlemen," "Dr Janet of Harley Street," etc. Crown 8vo, cloth, 6s.

[*Just out.*

NEW NOVEL BY ANNIE THOMAS (Mrs PENDER CUDLIP).

False Pretences. By the Author of "Allerton Towers," "That Other Woman," "Kate Valliant," "A Girl's Folly," etc., etc. Crown 8vo, cloth, 6s.

[*Second Edition.*

The *WORLD* says:—"Miss Annie Thomas has rarely drawn a character so cleverly as that of the false and scheming Mrs Colraine."

NEW NOVEL BY DR ARABELLA KENEALY.

Some Men are such Gentlemen. By the Author of "Dr Janet of Harley Street," "Molly and Her Man-o'-War," etc. Crown 8vo, cloth, 6s. With a Frontispiece. [*Fifth Edition.*

The *ACADEMY* says:—"We take up a book by Miss Arabella Kenealy confidently expecting to be amused, and in her latest work we are not disappointed. The story is so brightly written that our interest is never allowed to flag. The heroine, Lois Clinton, is sweet and womanly. . . . The tale is told with spirit and vivacity, and shows no little skill in its descriptive passages."
The *PALL MALL GAZETTE* says:—"A book to be read breathlessly from beginning to end. It is decidedly original . . . its vivid interest. The picture of the girl is admirably drawn. The style is bright and easy."
TRUTH says:—"Its heroine is at once original and charming."

NEW NOVEL BY DORA RUSSELL.

The Other Bond. By the Author of "A Hidden Chain," "A Country Sweetheart," "The Drift of Fate," etc. Crown 8vo, cloth, 6s. [*Third Edition.*

The *ATHENÆUM* on Miss Russell's Works, says:—"Miss Russell writes easily and well, and she has the gift of making her characters describe themselves by their dialogue, which is bright and natural."

NEW NOVEL BY L. T. MEADE.

A Life for a Love. By the Author of "The Medicine Lady," "A Soldier of Fortune," "In an Iron Grip," etc., etc. Crown 8vo, cloth, 6s. With a Frontispiece by Hal Hurst. [*Third Edition. Just out.*

The *DAILY TELEGRAPH* says:—"This thrilling tale. The plot is worked out with remarkable ingenuity. The book abounds in clever and graphic characterisation."

18 *Bouverie Street, Fleet Street, London.*

NEW NOVELS AND STORIES—*Continued.*
NEW NOVEL BY FLORENCE MARRYAT.

The Beautiful Soul. By the Author of "A Fatal Silence," "There is no Death," etc., etc. Crown 8vo, cloth, 6s.   [*Fourth Edition.*

The *GUARDIAN* says:—" We read the book with real pleasure and interest. . . . In Felecia Hetherington, Miss Marryat has drawn a really fine character, and has given her what she claims for her in the title, a beautiful soul."
The *WORLD* says:—"An entertaining and animated story. . . . One of the most lovable women to whom novel readers have been introduced."

Une Culotte: An Impossible Story of Modern Oxford. By "TIVOLI," Author of "A Defender of the Faith." With Illustrations by A. W. COOPER. Crown 8vo, cloth, 6s.   [*Second Edition.*

The *DAILY CHRONICLE* says:—"The book is full of funny things. The story is a screaming farce, and will furnish plenty of amusement."

The Vengeance of Medea. By EDITH GRAY WHEELWRIGHT. Crown 8vo, cloth, 6s.

The *WESTERN DAILY MERCURY* says:—"Miss Wheelwright has introduced several delightful characters, and produced a work which will add to her reputation. The dialogue is especially well written."

A Ruined Life. By EMILY ST CLAIR. Crown 8vo, cloth, 6s.

The *BIRMINGHAM GAZETTE* says:—"A powerful story developed with considerable dramatic skill and remarkable fervour."

The Westovers. By ALGERNON RIDGEWAY. Author of "Westover's Ward," "Diana Fontaine," etc. Crown 8vo, cloth, 6s.

The *GLASGOW HERALD* says:—"'The Westovers' is a clever book."

The Flaming Sword. Being an Account of the Extraordinary Adventures and Discoveries of Dr PERCIVAL in the Wilds of Africa. Written by Himself. Crown 8vo, cloth, 6s.

The *SPEAKER* says:—"Mr Rider Haggard himself has not imagined more wonderful things than those which befell Dr Percival and his friends."
The *LITERARY WORLD* says:—"Out-Haggards Haggard."

In Due Season. By AGNES GOLDWIN. Crown 8vo, cloth, 6s.

The *ACADEMY* says:—"Her novel is well written, it flows easily, its situations are natural, its men and women are real."

His Last Amour. By MONOPOLE. Crown 8vo, cloth, 6s.

The *GLASGOW HERALD* says:—"The story is unfolded with considerable skill, and the interest of the reader is not allowed to flag."

NEW NOVELS AND STORIES—*Continued.*

An Unknown Power. By CHARLES E. R. BELLAIRS
Crown 8vo, cloth, 6s.

The *BELFAST NORTHERN WHIG* says:—"From start to finish the reader's attention is never allowed to flag. The characters are drawn with considerable fidelity to life. The plot is original, and its developments well worked out."

NEW NOVEL BY GERTRUDE L. WARREN.

The Mystery of Hazelgrove. By GERTRUDE L. WARREN. Crown 8vo, cloth, 6s.   [*Just out.*

NEW NOVEL BY ALICE MAUD MEADOWS.

When the Heart is Young. By the Author of "The Romance of a Madhouse," etc. Crown 8vo, cloth. 6s.   [*Fourth Edition.*

A NEW AUSTRALIAN NOVEL.

Recognition. A Mystery of the Coming Colony. By SYDNEY H. WRIGHT. Crown 8vo, cloth, 6s. [*Shortly.*

A NEW SPORTING STORY.

With the Bankshire Hounds. By M. F. H. Crown 8vo, cloth, 6s.   [*Just out.*

Some Passages in Plantagenet Paul's Life. By HIMSELF. Crown 8vo, cloth, 6s.   [*Just out.*

Drifting. By MARSTON MOORE. Crown 8vo, cloth, 6s. [*Just out.*

Coneycreek. By M. LAWSON. Crown 8vo, cloth, 6s. [*Just out.*

IN THREE VOLUMES, Price **31s. 6d.**

BY DORA RUSSELL.

A Hidden Chain. By the Author of "Footprints in the Snow," "The Other Bond," etc., etc. In Three Volumes, crown 8vo, cloth, 31s. 6d. [*Second Edition.*

BY JEAN MIDDLEMASS.

The Mystery of Clement Dunraven. By the Author of "A Girl in a Thousand," etc. In Three Volumes, crown 8vo, cloth, 31s. 6d.   [*Second Edition.*

BY PERCY ROSS.

The Eccentrics. By the Author of "A Comedy without Laughter," "A Misguidit Lassie," "A Professor of Alchemy," etc. In Three Volumes, crown 8vo, cloth, 31s. 6d.

NEW NOVELS AND STORIES—*Continued.*

By GILBERTA M. F. LYON.

Absent Yet Present. By the Author of "For Good or Evil." In Three Volumes, crown 8vo, cloth, 31s. 6d.

By MADELINE CRICHTON.

Like a Sister. In Three Volumes, crown 8vo, cloth, 31s. 6d. [*Second Edition.*

IN ONE VOLUME, Price **3s. 6d.**

NEW BOOK by the AUTHOR of "A PLUNGE INTO SPACE."

The Crack of Doom. By ROBERT CROMIE, Author of "For England's Sake," etc. Crown 8vo, cloth, 3s. 6d.

*** The first Large Edition was exhausted before publication. SECOND EDITION now ready.

Her Loving Slave. By HUME NISBET, author of "The Jolly Roger," "Bail Up," etc., etc. In Handsome Pictorial Binding, with Illustrations by the Author. Crown 8vo, cloth, 3s. 6d. [*Third Edition.*

His Egyptian Wife. By HILTON HILL. Crown 8vo, cloth, 3s. 6d. With Frontispiece.

*** Published simultaneously in London and New York.

A Son of Noah. By MARY ANDERSON, author of "Othello's Occupation." Crown 8vo, cloth, 3s. 6d. [*Fifth Edition.*

The Last Cruise of the Teal. By LEIGH RAY. In handsome pictorial binding. Illustrated throughout. Crown 8vo, cloth, 3s. 6d. [*Second Edition.*

The *NATIONAL OBSERVER* says :—" It is long since we have lighted on so good a story of adventure."

His Troublesome Sister. By EVA TRAVERS EVERED POOLE, Author of many Popular Stories. Crown 8vo, cloth, 3s. 6d.

The *BIRMINGHAM POST* says :—"An interesting and well-constructed story. The characters are strongly drawn, the plot is well devised, and those who commence the book will be sure to finish it."

The Bow and the Sword. A Romance. By E. C. ADAMS, M.A. With 16 full-page drawings by MATTHEW STRETCH. Crown 8vo, pictorial cloth, 3s. 6d.

The *MORNING POST* says :—"The author reconstructs cleverly the life of one of the most cultivated nations of antiquity, and describes both wars and pageants with picturesque vigour. The illustrations are well executed."

NEW NOVELS AND STORIES—*Continued.*

The Maid of Havodwen. By JOHN FERRARS. Author of "Claud Brennan." Crown 8vo, cloth, 3*s.* 6*d.*

The *DUNDEE ADVERTISER* says :—"A charming story of Welsh life and character. . . . Deeply interesting. . . . Of unusual attractiveness."

Paths that Cross. By MARK TREHERN. Crown 8vo, cloth, 3*s.* 6*d.*

The *DAILY TELEGRAPH* says:—"Cleverly sketched characters. The book is enlivened throughout with innumerable light touches of quaint and spontaneous humour."

A Tale of Two Curates. By Rev. JAMES COPNER, M.A. Crown 8vo, cloth, 3*s.* 6*d.*

The *DUNDEE ADVERTISER* says:—"Simply but graphically narrated."

The Wrong of Fate. By LILLIAS LOBENHOFFER, Author of "Bairnie," etc. Crown 8vo, cloth, 3*s.* 6*d.*

The *LONDON STAR* says:—"A well-written and clever novel, excellent studies of Scotch character."
The *SCOTSMAN* says:—"Shows considerable power."

Studies in Miniature. By A TITULAR VICAR. Crown 8vo, cloth, 3*s.* 6*d.*

The *MANCHESTER COURIER* says :—"Brightly and cleverly written."
The *BELFAST NEWS LETTER* says :—"Very readable, characters admirably drawn."

Spunyarn. By N. J. PRESTON. Crown 8vo, pictorial cloth, 3*s.* 6*d.* [*Just out.*

IN ONE VOLUME, Price **2s. 6d.**

Lost! £100 Reward. By MIRIAM YOUNG, Author of "The Girl Musician." Crown 8vo, cloth, 2*s.* 6*d.*

The *WEEKLY SUN* says:—"The interest is well sustained throughout, and the incidents are most graphically described."

Clenched Antagonisms. By LEWIS IRAM. Crown 8vo, cloth, 2*s.* 6*d.*

The *SATURDAY REVIEW* says :—"'Clenched Antagonisms' is a powerful and ghastly narrative of the triumph of force over virtue. The book gives a striking illustration of the barbarous incongruities that still exist in the midst of an advanced civilisation."

For Marjory's Sake : A Story of South Australian Country Life. By Mrs JOHN WATERHOUSE. In handsome cloth binding, with Illustrations. Crown 8vo, cloth, 2*s.* 6*d.*

The *LITERARY WORLD* says:—"A delightful little volume, fresh and dainty, and with the pure, free air of Australian country parts blowing through it . . . gracefully told . . . the writing is graceful and easy."

IN ONE VOLUME, PAPER COVER, Price **1s.**

A Stock Exchange Romance. By BRACEBRIDGE HEMYNG, Author of "The Stockbroker's Wife," "Called to the Bar," etc., etc. Edited by GEORGE GREGORY. Crown 8vo, picture cover, 1s. (TENTH THOUSAND.)

Our Discordant Life. By ADAM D'HÉRISTAL. Crown 8vo, picture cover, 1s.

A Police Sergeant's Secret. By KILSYTH STELLIER, Author of "Taken by Force." Crown 8vo, picture cover, 1s. (FIFTH THOUSAND.)

Irish Stew. By JAMES J. MORAN, Author of "A Deformed Idol," "The Dunferry Risin'," "Runs in the Blood," etc. Crown 8vo, lithographed cover, price 1s.

The *WEEKLY SUN* says :—" Mr MORAN is the 'Barrie' of Ireland. . . . In a remote district in the west of Ireland he has created an Irish Thrums."

La Lecsinska. A Powerful and Clever Novel. By HARRIET BUCKLEY. Crown 8vo, paper cover, 1s.

[*Just out.*

That Other Fellow. An Original and Absorbing Novel. By Mrs LOUISA LE BAILLY. Crown 8vo, paper cover, 1s. [*Just out.*

DIGBY'S POPULAR NOVEL SERIES.

In Handsome Cloth Binding, Gold Lettered, Cr. 8vo, 320 pp. Price **2s. 6d.** *each, or in Picture Boards, Price* **2s.** *each.*

BY JEAN MIDDLEMASS.

THE MYSTERY OF CLEMENT DUNRAVEN. By the Author of "A Girl in a Thousand," etc. (SECOND EDITION.)

BY DR. A. KENEALY.

Dr JANET OF HARLEY STREET. By the Author of "Molly and her Man-o'-War," etc. (SEVENTH EDITION.) With Portrait.

BY DORA RUSSELL.

A HIDDEN CHAIN. By the Author of "Footprints in the Snow," etc. (SECOND EDITION.)

BY HUME NISBET.

THE JOLLY ROGER. By the Author of "Bail Up," etc. With Illustrations by the Author. (FIFTH EDITION.)

NOTE.—Other Works in the same Series in due course.

MISCELLANEOUS.

A History of the Great Western Railway from Its Inception to the Present Time.
By G. A. SEKON. Revised by F. G. SAUNDERS, Chairman of the Great Western Railway. Demy 8vo, 390 pages, cloth, 7s. 6d. With numerous Illustrations.

_{*} *Illustrated Prospectus, post free.* [*Second Edition.*

The *TIMES*, April 12th, 1895.—"Mr Sekon's volume is full of interest, and constitutes an important chapter in the history of railway development in England."

The *STANDARD* (Leader), April 4th, 1895.—"An excellent addition to the literature of our iron roads."

The *DAILY TELEGRAPH*, April 13th, 1895.—"Mr G. A. Sekon has performed a service to the public. His book is full of interest, and is evidently the result of a great deal of painstaking inquiry. . . . His book is made all the more valuable by several pictures of engines, collisions, the Saltash Bridge, the Old Bath Station and the Box Tunnel ; and it will be welcomed by all interested in the history and extraordinary expansion of our iron roadways."

Three Empresses. Josephine, Marie-Louise, Eugénie.
By CAROLINE GEAREY, Author of " In Other Lands," etc. With portraits. Cr. 8vo, cloth, 6s. (SECOND EDIT.)

The *PALL MALL GAZETTE* says:—" This charming book. . . . Gracefully and graphically written, the story of each Empress is clearly and fully told. . . This delightful book."

Winter and Summer Excursions in Canada.
By C. L. JOHNSTONE, Author of " Historical Families of Dumfriesshire," etc. With Illustrations. Crown 8vo, cloth, 6s.

The *DAILY NEWS* says:—" Not for a long while have we read a book of its class which deserves so much confidence. Intending settlers would do well to study Mr Johnstone's book."

The Author's Manual. By PERCY RUSSELL. With
Prefatory Remarks by Mr GLADSTONE. Crown 8vo, cloth, 3s. 6d. net. (EIGHTH AND CHEAPER EDITION.) With portrait.

The *WESTMINSTER REVIEW* says:—". . Mr Russell's book is a very complete manual and guide for journalist and author. It is not a merely practical work—it is literary and appreciative of literature in its best sense: . . . we have little else but praise for the volume."

A Guide to British and American Novels.
From the Earliest Period to the end of 1894. By PERCY RUSSELL, Author of "The Author's Manual," etc. Crown 8vo, cloth. Price 3s. 6d. net. (SECOND EDITION CAREFULLY REVISED.)

The *SPECTATOR* says:—" Mr Russell's familiarity with every form of novel is amazing, and his summaries of plots and comments thereon are as brief and lucid as they are various."

MISCELLANEOUS—*Continued.*

Sixty Years' Experience as an Irish Landlord.

Memoirs of JOHN HAMILTON, D.L. of St Ernan's Donegal. Edited, with Introduction, by the Rev. H C. WHITE, late Chaplain, Paris. Crown 8vo, cloth, 6s. With Portrait.

The *TIMES* says:—"Much valuable light on the real history of Ireland, and of the Irish agrarian question in the present century is thrown by a very interesting volume entitled 'Sixty Years' Experience as an Irish Landlord.' . . . This very instructive volume."

Nigh on Sixty Years at Sea. By ROBERT WOOL-

WARD ("Old Woolward"). Crown 8vo, cloth, 6s. With Portrait. (SECOND EDITION.)

The *TIMES* says:—"Very entertaining reading. Captain Woolward writes sensibly and straightforwardly, and tells his story with the frankness of an old salt. He has a keen sense of humour, and his stories are endless and very entertaining."

Whose Fault? The Story of a Trial at *Nisi Prius.*

By ELLIS J. DAVIS, Barrister-at-Law. In handsome pictorial binding. Crown 8vo, cloth, 3s. 6d.

The *TIMES* says:—"An ingenious attempt to convey to the lay mind an accurate and complete idea of the origin and progress and all the essential circumstances of an ordinary action at law. The idea is certainly a good one, and is executed in very entertaining fashion. . . . Mr Davis's instructive little book."

Borodin and Liszt. I.—Life and Works of a Russian

Composer. II.—Liszt, as sketched in the Letters of Borodin. By ALFRED HABETS. Translated with a Preface by ROSA NEWMARCH. With Portraits and Fac-similes.   [*Just out.*

Fragments from Victor Hugo's Legends and

Lyrics. By CECILIA ELIZABETH MEETKERKE. Crown 8vo, cloth, 7s. 6d.

The *WORLD* says:—"The most admirable rendering of French poetry into English that has come to our knowledge since Father Prout's translation of 'La Chant du Cosaqne.'"

BY THE AUTHOR OF "SONG FAVOURS."

Minutiæ. By CHARLES WILLIAM DALMON. Royal

16mo, cloth elegant, price 2s. 6d.

The *ACADEMY* says:—"His song has a rare and sweet note. The little book has colour and fragrance, and is none the less welcome because the fragrance is delicate, evanescent; the colours of white and silver grey and lavender, rather than brilliant and exuberant. . . . Mr Dalmon's genuine artistry. In his sonnets he shows a deft touch, particularly in the fine one, 'Ecce Ancilla Domini.' Yet, after all, it is in the lyrics that he is most individual. . . . Let him take heart, for surely the song that he has to sing is worth singing."

*** *A complete Catalogue of Novels, Travels, Biographies, Poems, etc., with a critical or descriptive notice of each, free by post on application.*

London: **DIGBY, LONG & CO.**, Publishers,
18 *Bouverie Street, Fleet Street, E.C.*

www.ingramcontent.com/pod-product-compliance
Lightning Source LLC
Chambersburg PA
CBHW030109030726
47498CB00007B/2311